Praise for Shelley Bradley's *Naughty Little Secret*

5 out of 5! "Warning! This novel may cause heart palpitations, sweating, and tears. Ice chips and a cold shower recommended! Shelley Bradley takes the reader on a whirlwind of emotions throughout NAUGHTY LITTLE SECRET. Highly erotic and extremely tender at the same time, this book made me smile, cry, and squirm in my seat. This one is definitely a keeper." ~ *Natasha, Romance Junkies*

5 out of 5! "With humorously witty dialog and some very graphic sex, the readers are in for a very decadent treat as Bradley packs a wallop with this extremely sensual, well done read. Additionally, when you couple all that with the bonus of a tender love story you end up with a very stimulating and satisfying story." – *Marilyn, Ck2s Kwips and Kritiques*

5 out of 5! "NAUGHTY LITTLE SECRET is an amazing book. I could feel the emotions vibrating throughout. I devoured each word…" ~ *Shayla, Romance Junkies*

"NAUGHTY LITTLE SECRET is not only erotic, but also sexy and sensual. Shelley Bradley knows exactly what her readers want and she skillfully provides it. The intensity of the sexual attraction between these two characters is unrelenting and you'll undoubtedly be swept away on the tide of their desire. The scene in which Noah is "revealed" is quite possibly one of the most erotic, emotion-filled scenes ever written." ~ *Two Lips Reviews*

"NAUGHTY LITTLE SECRET by Shelley Bradley is utterly fantastic! With its fast pace, engaging plot and super sizzling sex, Naughty Little Secret is an indulgence you won't want to miss." ~ *Joyfully Reviewed*

Naughty Little Secret

Shelley Bradley

A SAMHAIN PUBLISHING, LTD. publication.

Samhain Publishing, Ltd.
2932 Ross Clark Circle, #384
Dothan, AL 36301
www.samhainpublishing.com

Naughty Little Secret
Copyright © 2006 by Shelley Bradley, LLC
Print ISBN: 1-59998-293-5
Digital ISBN: 1-59998-162-9

Editing by Angie James
Cover by Scott Carpenter

First Samhain Publishing, Ltd. electronic publication: August 2006
First Samhain Publishing, Ltd. print publication: November 2006

Dedication

A big thanks to all the Ladies of the Forum for your support, encouragement and love. Lora, Susan, Janine, Gloria, Connie, Joy, Natalie, Sheila—all of you are the wildest, sweetest bunch of ladies!

Special thanks to Annmarie for reading. Multiple drafts. Answering questions. Many of them. And not losing her patience or enthusiasm once. You're a gem!

Chapter One

"Lauren?"

His voice haunted her... So deep it vibrated inside her, heating her libido up faster than anything requiring batteries. Low and controlled, like he was murmuring to a lover, making sure she knew everything he planned to do to her body. She could hear him now in her head.

I'm going to strip you down to your skin, sugar, and kiss you until you can't remember taking a breath you don't share with me. Then I'm going to test just how wet you are. With my tongue. Before I spend the night inside you, making you scream my name...

"Lauren?"

Oh, his voice... The man could make her wet with a simple hello. His killer voice had a hint of gruffness that suggested he was coming off an all-nighter of sweaty, amazing sex.

Then again, maybe he was...with his endless string of twenty-something Barbie dolls.

"Lauren?"

She blinked, coming back to his cluttered office and her hour-old coffee. The recurring fantasies of Noah Reeves had to stop. She wasn't his type—at all. At thirty-six, Lauren had given up on Miss Clairol and let her faux golden streaks turn a natural caramel. Her infrequent trips to the gym probably weren't enough to keep her ass from spreading.

She sighed. Somehow, in the last ten years, she felt like she'd become Barbie's frumpy Aunt Gertrude.

Men like Noah didn't desire Gertrude. Or sleep with them. She needed a serious reality check if she thought for an instant that he'd seen her as anything but an employee for the past year. To him, she was just a staff manager for the growing chain of upscale steakhouses he owned with four other men.

And his old buddy's ex-wife.

Too bad she was having a damn hard time thinking of him as anything other than a fantasy.

She glanced again at Noah. One little peek couldn't hurt, right?

Big mistake. Sin on a stick. Calendar hunky with spiked dark hair, eyes somewhere between blue and gray, ruthlessly carved cheekbones, and shoulders so wide they induced drool. The whispered rumors about him did nothing to cool her down. She'd heard the man was a serious powerhouse in bed—big, built, and not afraid to use every inch God gave him. Dominant. Noah was seriously hot.

Once. Just once, she'd like to know what it was like to get down and dirty with a man like him. Wine-drenched fantasies of Noah ordering her to the bed, demanding she spread her legs, then becoming master of all he surveyed… Lauren could get off to that vision in about three minutes. She'd timed it.

And if she didn't stop mooning over her boss and start focusing on her job, she was going to be unemployed.

"I asked if you have the site visit reports." He frowned, concern softening his gaze. "Are you okay?"

"Fine. Just fine." As long as she kept the heavy breathing to a minimum, anyway.

"You sure? You look awfully flushed."

Damn, why wouldn't the earth open up and swallow her whole? She'd been imagining him naked and aroused and ready to claim her. She'd even worn her sexiest short skirt and a sheer blouse that showed a hint of cleavage. His reaction? He'd spent most of the day looking elsewhere. And now, he was thinking about a report she generated yesterday.

Why had she thought it was a good idea to test Noah's reactions to her charms? Again?

She'd kidded herself a few weeks ago that maybe she'd been too subtle in her attempt to get his attention. Her second attempt had gone largely unnoticed, as he'd had off-site meetings most of that day. The fifteen minutes she had seen him, of course, hadn't been enough time for him to notice her. But today, closeted in his office, just the two of them, she wore a damn near see-through blouse and total fuck-me shoes, and he was still determined to look anywhere but at her. Lauren sighed. Time to face reality. All signs pointed to Noah being immune to her.

"Sorry," she murmured, mentally slapping herself. "I'm not feeling very well."

"You need to lie down for a minute?"

Lauren held in a groan. She'd love to ask if he'd mind lying down with her and helping her out with the cobwebs surely lining her vagina since she'd been divorced and without for two years...but she just wasn't up for the humiliation of his polite refusal.

And it would be oh-so-polite. Noah was not just yummy but nice. The total package, in fact. Looks, brains, kindness, a sometimes shy-boy sparkle she'd always liked.

The concern on his face was so genuine—a furrow of brow, a sharp assessment of those wintery blue eyes. He reached out to touch her shoulder, then apparently changed his mind.

The man couldn't even bring himself to touch her? Ugh, humiliating!

She shook her head. "I'm fine. I have copies of the site reports on my desk. I can run and get them…"

Noah raised a tanned forearm, visible under the rolled-up cuff of his dress shirt, and checked his watch. "I didn't realize it was so late. What do you say we break for lunch?"

We? Lauren perked up. Was he asking her out to lunch?

"I know a great little place a few miles from here. Awesome sandwiches. I can drive."

Noah hesitated, and Lauren nearly cringed at his considering expression. Lord, he hadn't been asking her out. When would she get a clue? He'd merely been suggesting they needed a break from work.

"I was just thinking that we could bring some of our work with us and keep talking, but we can reconvene at two, if you'd rather." She shrugged with affected nonchalance.

And hoped to hell he bought her indifferent routine.

"Meeting back here at two works for me, actually. I have…an errand to run."

Hmm. She'd bet his "errand" was named Misty, a bombshell in her mid-twenties he'd started dating a few months ago. Misty was, of all things, a professional cheerleader. It was all Lauren could do not to snort. Professional cheerleader. Yeah, no doubt Noah was going to spend his lunch hour shaking her pom-poms.

"You'll be okay alone?" he asked gently.

Sure. She'd been alone for the last two years—longer, really. Tim, her ex, hadn't been with her for the last five years of their marriage. Noah, his old college pal and her current boss, wasn't likely to volunteer to fill the void. First, men had that "buddy" line they didn't cross. Sisters and wives were off limits. She was learning the hard way it apparently applied to ex-wives, too. Second, even if he had been interested, she wasn't in the market for a relationship. Happily ever after just wasn't in the cards for her, and she wasn't in the mood to endure the pain and humiliation of a break up again. A tidy little fling would be just fine, thank you very much. Except Noah wasn't cooperating.

Probably just as well. Noah was the kind of man she could seriously fall for—even if she didn't want to. And he was all about lovin' èm and leavin' èm. She didn't want to be left. Been there, done that. Hell, she'd made the T-shirt.

And Noah would definitely break her heart if she let him.

"Fine. I have some phone calls to return and...stuff to do. I'll see you back here in an hour."

Before he could say another word, Lauren rose, tugged on her embarrassingly short skirt, and hustled out of his office.

Back at her desk, she took a deep breath and squeezed her thighs together. So much for mere friendship. Being beside Noah for the better part of four hours had made her achy and wet, despite the fact they'd discussed nothing more exciting than ongoing construction and possible new restaurant sites. If the man ever talked dirty to her, she'd probably flood her panties. And have an orgasm from his voice alone.

The fantasies she'd been spinning of a naked Noah hadn't helped. A glance down proved her nipples stood straight out, in full salute. He couldn't have missed them.

Lauren sighed. No, he'd noticed. She'd seen him glance in her direction once or twice. But he'd looked away quickly. They hadn't mattered. *She* didn't matter, not sexually. Not to him.

Just her luck.

Lauren had no one to blame but herself. It never failed. She'd taken an interest in a man who just didn't want her. Men who asked her out, like the new guy in Accounting, Gary, never interested her. Never. What the hell was wrong with her?

She wasn't going to solve that riddle in the next sixty minutes, so she grabbed her keys and her purse and headed out of Tender Fork's offices, through the building's shared lobby, then out to her car.

Noah's parking space already sat empty. Apparently, he couldn't wait to do his "errand"—or rather, to do Misty.

Lauren held back unexpected tears. *Rah freakin' rah…*

ରେ ରେ ରେ

An hour later, Lauren returned to Noah's office. He sat waiting for her, looking a little disheveled, a forgotten sandwich at his elbow. Apparently, his little cheerleader had spent the last hour with her hands mussing up his hair while he, no doubt, had completely sated her. After such great sex, who cared about something as mundane as turkey on wheat with sprouts?

When she sat at the small round table on the other side of his office and dragged out her folder, Noah's head shot up.

He smiled, clearing his throat, then quickly looked away. "Good lunch?"

Fabulous. I met four marines in the parking lot at Denny's and we went for it. You? "Um, fine."

"Feeling better?"

"Fine. Let's just finish this. I know you have another meeting, and I promised Emma I'd be on time tonight so I can take her to her dance class."

Surprise furrowed Noah's brow. "On a Wednesday? I thought Emma's class was on Saturday."

It was Lauren's turn to be surprised. He'd remembered the day of Emma's ballet lesson after a passing comment? Well, why not? The man was a genius, and his mind frankly amazed her.

"The kids are with Tim this weekend, and he's planning to take them up to the lake. This is Emma's make up lesson."

"What are your plans this weekend?"

Lauren paused. Did Noah want to know as a man or a boss? Had to be the latter. Why would he be interested in her when he had Misty and her pom-poms?

"I'm going to try finishing laying the tile in the bathroom floor. I'm close now. It'll be nice to have that chore done."

She would not ask him about his plans. No doubt it would be something involving Misty and satin sheets. Lauren would rather not know.

Sad, really. She hadn't always been this way around Noah. When she'd been newly married to Tim, before the high-powered job and the kids and the PTA meetings consumed their lives, she'd enjoyed Noah's great company and sharp wit, and hoped he'd find the right woman someday. Now, she suspected if he announced he'd found the right

13

woman, Lauren would feel an irrational urge to break her legs. She'd never even met Misty, and already she didn't like her.

"Hmm," he responded. "Since I have nothing planned, I assumed whatever you had going on had to be more exciting, but clearly, I'm wrong."

Nope. But it could be exciting if you wanted to lay me, rather than me laying the tile floor... "You mean you don't want to play house?" she teased.

As soon as the words left her mouth, she could have slapped herself. Oh, that comment had come out so wrong...

"I—I meant help me finish the girls' bathroom."

Noah looked like he might be repressing a smile. "Um...no. Sorry. Enjoy, though."

"Leaving all the fun to me, huh? I can't wait." Sarcasm dripped from her tone.

This was the rapport with Noah she missed. Fun chitchat, the banter back and forth. They hadn't been able to just talk like this since...well, since just before the divorce, when she'd really started looking at him as a man. And wanting him. He remained friends with Tim, but had reached out to her soon after the split and told her that if she needed anything, he would help. And he had, with a great job. But their easy camaraderie of the past was nearly non-existent.

When she glanced at him again, he shot her a mischievous smile and a very direct stare. While it rarely dropped below her neck, Lauren sure felt it right between her legs. His gaze did all kinds of damage to her self-control. If she didn't know better, she'd think he might be...flirting? No. Wishful thinking.

Business, not bedroom play.

Lauren should look away, knew she should. Only Noah's blue eyes reeled her in. The man was mesmerizing. And she had to stop gawking and drooling or he'd know how badly she wanted to jump him. Hell, he might even fire her for sexual harassment.

"Only three items left on our list of things to cover," she said, breaking the tense silence with an all-business comment.

"Three things. Hmm." He turned his attention to his computer.

Finally, she could breathe again.

Noah grabbed his mouse, long, strong fingers curling around the oblong plastic. Lauren would rather see them elsewhere. Like on her.

Give it up and get over it. She sighed and returned to the notes in her folder.

"Lauren, I can't find the email you sent with those new appetizer reports. You know, the ones you put out last week? Can you print me another copy?"

"Sure," she said, happy for an excuse to leave the weird air swirling between them. Entirely her imagining, she was sure.

When Lauren rounded the corner of her desk, she moved to sit in her chair…and found something in it. A textured white envelope. Nothing written on the front, but definitely something inside, judging from the bulge of neatly-folded paper.

Given the fact it was on her chair, she assumed someone set it here for her. Safe assumption, right?

Shrugging, she opened the envelope, withdrew the lone page inside, and unfolded the thick paper.

You. Me. Naked skin. Shared fantasies. A whole night.
Soon.

Lauren blinked at the typed note. Read it again. And nearly stopped breathing. Someone here wanted her? Someone who'd gone to the trouble of writing her a note and leaving it in her chair. No hint of a signature or his identity. And maybe the situation should have creeped her out...but she didn't sense menace behind the words, just desire.

She looked around the sea of cubicles with new eyes. Who? Gary was too straightforward. Most of the other men here were older, happily married, or gay. Except Noah, and he had little Miss Pompoms to keep him warm at night. Maybe it was simply someone who worked in the building. Tender Forks shared this building with several other businesses. Security was relaxed. Maybe it was one of the consultants across the hall? The possibility didn't excite her.

"Lauren?"

The object of her fantasies stopped just behind her, his deep, sin-inspiring voice seeping into her. His warm breath cascaded down the back of her neck. She couldn't help it; she shivered. "You find that report?"

"Report?" she repeated numbly.

She couldn't seem to get her mind off a whole night of naked skin and shared fantasies and inserting Noah in the picture.

"This it?" He took the piece of paper from her hand and lifted it to read.

Lauren reached out to grab the page back, but it was too late. His dark expression told her he'd already read every word.

"Did someone give this to you?"

She could feel herself flushing every shade of red. "I found it in my chair. Someone left it there."

"Interesting note."

She couldn't tell whether he was pissed she might be hooking up with someone in the office or so amused he was about to laugh his ass off. He was a master negotiator. His face never gave away anything unless he wanted it to.

"I—I don't know who left it."

"Well, you don't have to guess what he wants."

The flush spread wider, seeping heat through her body. "No, that's clear."

He quirked a dark brow at her. "Worried? Do you think this is some psycho? I can beef up security."

Gnawing on her bottom lip, she cast a brief glance up at Noah. Those gorgeous blue eyes were too much to look at, her desire too deep to conceal from him. She looked away.

How perfect. One man wanted her—a man who clearly understood how much she loved surprises and wished for a lover. But the man she ached for stood right in front of her, asking questions and offering to protect her like a brother. Damn, he chased everything else in a skirt. Why not her?

"I'm fine. You need that appetizer report, right?" She moved to round the corner of her desk, toward her computer.

Noah grabbed her arm, his grip gentle but unyielding. "Talk to me. Are you scared?"

With a rueful smile, she worked to set him at ease. "I probably should be. But this is the most admiration I've had since my divorce. Whoever it is, I don't think he means any harm."

Slowly, he released her arm and sent her a long stare. "You want naked skin and shared fantasies?"

Lauren sighed. "What red-blooded woman doesn't? I appreciate your concern, but—"

"Can you handle skin and fantasies?"

She shrugged, wondering if Noah cared even a tiny bit that some other man wanted to hold her. "According to him, I'll find out soon. Guess I'll let you know then."

Chapter Two

TGIF! Lauren was more than ready to call it a week. After Wednesday's fiasco with the short skirt and filmy blouse, she almost thanked the unexpected cold front that forced her to wear wool pants and a cashmere sweater on Thursday. Or she would have been happy, if she hadn't realized that the more clothes she wore, the more comfortable Noah seemed to be.

Grateful for casual Friday, today Lauren wore no-nonsense jeans and sneakers and a turtleneck. She sighed. Only a nun's habit was more asexual.

She glanced at her watch as she made her way back to her desk from a meeting so boring, watching paint peel sounded positively thrilling in comparison. 3:45 p.m. An hour and fifteen minutes. Sorting through the rest of her email today would take up that time. Then…she'd have a whole weekend to herself.

And she was determined to spend it thinking about anything and anyone except Noah Reeves.

As Lauren approached her desk, she immediately saw a pristine rectangular box with a big red bow sitting on top of all the clutter. A red rose lay across the lid.

She hesitated, frowning, and looked around. No one stood nearby. Her desk was in a corner, near the window. There was no way someone had accidentally left this here. It had been specifically placed on her desk, where she couldn't possibly miss it.

By the person who'd left the bare skin and fantasies note the day before yesterday?

Biting her lip, she approached the box and picked it up, setting the rose aside. Light. A little smaller than a shirt box. It bore the markings of a posh lingerie store not far from the office, where she'd window shopped many times. But she couldn't justify actually buying anything there, given the fact no one would see the sweet nothings except her. And maybe an EMT or two if she ever got into an accident.

A curious anticipation settled in her belly. In truth, she should be scared. If this was the same guy who'd written the note, he was starting to look serious. That excited more than scared her. After being sexually invisible to Tim for years and being certain the opposite sex regarded her as a mom/fellow football fan, a little sexual attention felt nicer than she ought to admit to.

With her heart picking up its pace, Lauren tugged on the silky red ribbon. It unraveled under her fingers, slithering to the desk in silence. She lifted the lid and read the typed note sitting on top of the crisp pink tissue paper.

You. Me. Naked skin. Shared fantasies. A whole night.
Tonight.

The same note as Wednesday, but he'd changed *soon* to *tonight.* As in after work tonight? Would he just…reveal himself? Call her? Maybe the box held answers.

Her pulse picked up a bit more speed as she broke the golden seal holding the tissue paper closed and peeled back the delicate pieces.

Holy cow!

If the note hadn't spelled it out, Lauren would get a very clear idea of what Mr. Mysterious had in mind now from the contents of this box. The two items inside were red lace and small. Scratch that. Red lace and very small.

She picked up one. A red thong, soft and delicate. It would caress her body—what little it covered—in silken seduction. She didn't even need to pick up the other item to see it was a red lace camisole with velvet laces up the front. And underwire support. A glance at the tag had her jaw dropping. Her secret admirer had guessed her bra size perfectly.

"Do a little shopping in preparation for the weekend?" drawled a familiar raspy-sexy voice behind her. "If so, I'm guessing you found something more exciting to do than lay tile."

With a gasp, she shoved the lingerie back in the box and closed the lid. "Did you need something?"

"Eventually. First, I want the answer to my question."

Lauren started chewing on her lip again, torn between hiding the truth and complete embarrassment. He seemed…amused. A heartbeat away from laughing.

This was so not funny. Just because he didn't find her attractive didn't mean no one else would.

"No. As a matter of fact, the admirer who left the note on Wednesday left this while I was at my last meeting."

21

"Tenacious. I'll give him that." Noah stroked his chin. "And you have no idea who it is?"

"I don't," she admitted. "But after spending the kind of money to buy this little…ensemble at Seductions and Secrets, I don't think he'll be a stranger much longer."

"You okay with that? After the divorce—"

"It's been two years, Noah. I know you and Tim are pals and all, but it's really no longer any of his business what I do with my time."

"Agreed." He held up his hands to ward off any further tirades. "So, is red your color?"

Oh, yeah. Sinful, sexual, siren red. "Why not? Do I not look like a red sort of woman?" she challenged. "You probably think I'm all white cotton, and you're wrong."

The full line of his mouth twitched, as if he might be fighting a smile, before his expression smoothed.

"I'm pleading the fifth." He frowned. "How did this guy know your size? Assuming he even got it right."

Lauren hesitated. "Well…I don't know. But the size is perfect, so I'm guessing he knows his way around a woman's body."

"You sure you can handle this? You don't want me to have security look into the situation?"

She felt her blood pressure rise. Hell, rise—it skyrocketed. "Thank you for the intimation that the only man who could want me must be a psycho."

"I didn't say he was a psycho. Even if he's not, most men are sexually demanding, Lauren. This sounds like someone who wants to tie you down, fill you up with everything he's got, and take you for a long, hard ride."

"And your point is…? Noah, I'm divorced, not a virgin." Gritting her teeth, she pulled away from him, stomping around the corner of her desk.

He grabbed her and brought her back around to face him. "You want to find yourself on your knees with a mouthful of cock or be introduced to the back of the couch when he bends you over it to fuck you?"

His words flooded her with heat. She pictured herself before Noah, kneeling at his feet, looking up into his familiar, rugged face as he grabbed her hair and led her mouth to his waiting cock. She'd lick the head, drag her tongue all down the shaft, then suck him deep and feel him fist his hands in her hair and groan, demanding more.

"Your pupils are dilating. You like that idea?"

Lauren took a deep breath, watching his unreadable face with hot eyes and resisting the urge to press her thighs together. Oh, God. She was getting hot having a conversation with her boss. And if he knew he starred in her little X-rated daydreams, he'd probably run in the other direction. She needed to watch her tongue and her temper—and her runaway fantasies.

"I don't want to talk about it. Did you need something, sir?"

Impatience skated across his features. "Lauren, answer me."

"Please, just forget it." This whole argument was too humiliating for words.

He sat on a corner of her desk. By virtue of his six-three frame, he towered over her as he braced his elbow on one knee and leaned closer to her. Not for the first time, Lauren wished her sense of smell was something more than non-existent. She'd bet Noah's scent was yummy.

"Lauren, I'm sorry if I've upset you. I didn't intend to. I just wanted to make sure you know what you're getting into. Do you?"

"I'm familiar with the concept of sex. I have two children."

Noah grabbed the note. "I don't think this guy is talking about some civilized little screw. He's talking possession. Are you comfortable with being completely taken? If you're uneasy, I'll do what I can to stop him."

The anger drained out of her. As always, nice. Polite, more or less. She couldn't look at him and say what was on the tip of her tongue. But it had to be said.

"Look." She sighed and stared at the half-closed box in her lap—not at him. "I'm a grown woman. I may not be twenty-five anymore and I may not be a professional cheerleader, but I still like to feel desired."

Noah groaned. "Lauren—"

"Save the speech. I haven't had any attention from a man in a lot of years, and it feels…nice. You're right. This guy may be off kilter. He may demand more than I want to give sexually. If so, I know how to say no. But I doubt I'll get in over my head. For now, I'm going to enjoy the fact someone has noticed I'm female. Can we drop it now?"

"One more question, then I'll shut up." At her reluctant nod, he hesitated. She'd bet he was choosing his words with care. He often did. In fact, he planned everything.

At least he was trying not to piss her off this time.

"I've known you a lot of years. Sometimes, you're an impulsive woman."

Hell, she could already hear him trying to talk her out of a fling with the mysterious lingerie-giving stranger. "The question, Noah?"

"You've had, what, two dates since your divorce? And now you're contemplating something way beyond dinner and a movie with someone you've never even met. Do you think you should take it slower?"

That did it! Her temper returned with a vengeance, spiking through her blood. She grabbed her purse, the gift box, and stood. "You've been counting my dates now like some older brother with a whacked-out daddy complex? It's been two years. You don't wait two weeks between one model and the next, but I need to go slow? Amazing."

Before five or not, she was leaving. The humiliation of this conversation was just too much.

She turned away and marched toward the door.

Noah restrained her by wrapping a hand around her elbow and drawing her closer. "You really want to wear red lace wisps for a guy you don't even know. You want to allow a stranger to touch you? To fuck you?"

Lauren jerked away, determined not to notice how her arm burned where he touched her or the body heat rolling off him in knee-weakening waves. "I want to feel alive again. I'm ready to get on with my life now. I'm ready to touch and be touched—"

Tears tightened her throat and she couldn't go on. God, she was baring her soul to a man who thought of her like a little sister. And until she'd spoken the words, Lauren hadn't realized how much she ached to have someone hold her. Tonight.

"Lauren… Sugar, I'm sorry if I upset you."

She shook her head, frowning to ward off more tears. "I'm fine. I just need to go."

Slowly, with obvious reluctance, he released her. "Sure. Where are you off to?"

Sending a pained smile in his direction, she held up the box. "I'm going home, put this stuff on, and get on with the rest of my life. Maybe Mr. Mysterious will show up and put a smile on my face."

CR CR CR

Cursing the dark shadows enshrouding the porch, Noah Reeves lifted the clay pot at his feet, now riot with a profusion of spring flowers that nearly made him sneeze—which would likely wake half the neighborhood. He managed to hold it in while he felt around the cold cement. Finally, his fingers latched onto metal. Just where it had always been… A grin broke out across his face as he grabbed the key and replaced the flowerpot.

After pocketing the key, Noah reached for the small black bag he'd set at his feet. He unzipped it slowly, silently. Barely restraining his impatience. Adrenaline crashed through his system as he extracted the leather gloves he'd packed, fished out the key again, and donned the gloves.

With leather-clad hands and a cock that wouldn't stand down, he opened the door.

Dark. Silence. Toward the back of the house, he saw a gray light casting down the hall, first bright, then dim, before turning bright once more. The TV, he'd bet. Damn, it was one in the morning. He'd have to work around it.

Reaching into his bag again, Noah pulled out his black ski mask and pulled it over his head. *Showtime…*

Palms sweating under his gloves and perspiration breaking out across his back, he crept down the hall toward the oddly flashing light. Slowly. Quietly. Heart threatening to pound out of his chest, Noah gripped the handle of his bag, breath held, as he neared his destination.

He'd waited nearly ten years for this opportunity. Ten fucking years. He'd plotted this night for the last two. Thought he'd die of impatience the last six months. And tonight…he could barely rein in his excitement or need. The urge to fuck, to claim, seized him. The now he'd been craving had finally arrived.

Noah reached the end of the hallway and peeked in. And nearly stopped breathing. She was here. Hopefully asleep. Alone.

All his.

Tip-toeing into the bedroom, Noah stared down at his fantasy, his future.

For now, she lay on her side, one hand under her flushed cheek, her pale thighs tangled up in her covers. The rest of her…almost totally exposed. Skin. Inches and inches of blessedly bare limbs, torso, and shoulders. The only covering? A familiar red lace thong and matching camisole. As he'd known the first time he'd seen the garments, Lauren looked delicious in them.

That was exactly why he'd bought them. And sent them to her. Then stopped to watch her blush and squirm once she opened them. And he'd been so damn hard imagining her in them ever since.

It's also why he played devil's advocate with her when she received them…to make sure she wasn't scared. To make sure she was ready—really ready—to let go of the past and take a lover.

Persuading her he should be that someone was the trick.

27

Noah hated subterfuge. This James Bond crap of sneaking in her house, pretending to be someone else, and surprising her wasn't his first choice. But he had to do something—fast.

Lauren had started dressing sexier at work. Last Wednesday, he'd nearly drooled on her—in between being mentally rushed by a thousand heady fantasies, all revolving around Lauren naked with her nails in his back while he pounded deep inside her. He'd had to look away to avoid jumping on her. Worse, he was pretty sure she'd worn the heart attack-inducing little skirt for Gary, the accounting twerp. Gary, who he wished had never been hired. Would she really go out with the guy? Sleep with him?

Not if Noah could help it. He'd waited ten years to have her. Gritted his teeth through two pregnancies and a rocky marriage to a guy who had never appreciated her as he should have. Tim wasn't a total jerk, just self-absorbed. Lauren deserved more.

Now, Noah was here to show her who he was, aside from having been Tim's college pal. She had to experience him in a way not related to the past, having nothing to do with being her boss. To see how she could be with him and no ex-husbands, business meetings—or clothes—between them.

Once he had her sated…then they'd talk. He'd reveal himself. And hope like hell she could admit to the something sizzling between them. He'd build on that. She knew he wasn't a selfish workaholic like Tim, but she had to understand that he'd devote himself to her pleasure and happiness. She liked and respected him. They connected intellectually, shared plenty in common, such as a quirky sense of humor. But Lauren thought of him as her surrogate big brother/Tim's Doberman. He had to change her opinion.

Starting tonight.

Blood whipped through his veins, lashed him with heat, as he stepped into the nearly quiet bedroom and made his way across the shadowy space. The sounds of canned sitcom laughter, with the volume turned very low, reached his ears. *Damn thing better not wake her*, he thought with a scowl.

She'd changed the furniture since Tim's departure. Good. Even if the house was the same, for the girls' sake, she'd replaced more intimate reminders of her marriage. In place of the Spartan mission style furniture they'd had before, Lauren had bought pieces that looked feminine, golden warm, and stylishly weathered. An intricate wrought-iron headboard made him smile.

All the curves and curls in that wrought-iron design would come in handy. Soon.

He reached her side, eased the bag onto the carpeted floor, and took a moment to contemplate the feast of female as he stared down into her peaceful face. Silvery tracks glistened on her cheek. Noah's smile fell. Had she been…crying?

He sank to his knees and looked closely. Yes, she had. The tears had fallen down her cheeks and dried as she'd drifted off. Even now, he could see her eyes were puffy, her nose a bit red.

The sight hit him like a battering ram to the gut. If the tears had anything to do with her girls or anything else she held dear, he'd hold her and help her find a way to make it better. If it had anything to do with Mr. Mysterious, as she put it, failing to put in an appearance…well, he'd soothe her ache—right now.

Noah fished a pair of velvet-lined cuffs from his bag and gently slipped one around Lauren's sleep-lax wrist. He frowned in concentration, his heart pounding like a turbo-charged sledgehammer into his chest. The next wrist, still tucked under her cheek, would prove more of a challenge. He had to do it without waking her. He couldn't risk her panicking, thinking she had a burglar or rapist, and possibly hurting herself.

While pondering the best way to move Lauren, she helped him out and rolled to her back.

He nearly swallowed his tongue. The red lace of the camisole hugged the curves of her breasts. The little velvet laces could barely contain her. Soft, round flesh spilled over the cups, tempting him with the pounding need to get on top of her, get deep inside of her, make sure she knew she was his.

*One thing at a time...*he reminded himself. Secure her, then fuck her. Waiting wasn't an option. He'd already done plenty of that.

Carefully, he reached for Lauren's other wrist and brought it up to the waiting cuff he'd fed through one of the iron headboard's curves. In response, she moaned, fidgeted, and pressed her thighs together. She wriggled her hips, then lifted them in his direction. Another moan, this one longer, lower, left her lush mouth. He started sweating again.

Shit! Even in her sleep, the woman tested his control.

With a muted click, Noah secured Lauren's wrist in the cuff. He released a breath he hadn't realized he'd been holding.

Everything was going according to plan. Lauren was ready sexually. If her body was available, her heart couldn't be far behind. Her kids were gone for the night. He'd had gifts delivered. Her curiosity—and hopefully more—was aroused. And now, he had her bound to the bed, ready for anything and everything he planned to give her. All according to schedule.

Tension squeezed his gut tight and engorged his cock even more as Noah tied a little black blindfold over her eyes and reached for the remote control. With the press of a button, the TV turned off, plunging the room into dark silence. Nearly ready, he pulled off his mask and gloves. Perfect.

Gritting his teeth against the urge to rip off his clothes and get inside her now, Noah settled for leaning down and kissing his way from the swells of her breasts, up to her neck, then nibbling on her lobe.

God, she smelled good. Clean. Like female sprinkled in…vanilla and musk. Something so her. Something siren sexy but not artificial. Lauren was too real to wear a lot of perfume. But her natural scent alone was enough to make him grit his teeth against the zipper and black denim strangling his cock.

She stirred, shifted, moaned.

"That's it," he whispered. "Wake up."

For an electric moment, she froze, now alert. Then she stiffened and lunged against the handcuffs.

Noah touched a tender hand to the center of her chest, holding her in place. With his other hand, he caressed her shoulder.

When she opened her mouth to scream, he covered it and whispered into her ear, "I promised you naked skin and fantasies. Tonight. The whole night. Are you ready?"

Chapter Three

Lauren froze, the unfamiliar whisper echoing in her ears. The pounding of her heart almost drowned the sound out. Almost...but she could still hear him breathing. Hard.

As he leaned against her, she could tell that his breathing wasn't the only thing hard.

Oh. My. God. The stranger was in her house. In her bed. Suddenly, she was terrified. She tried to remember everything she'd ever read about serial killers and rapists. But she was blank, rushed by a dousing of cold panic.

Half his body lay over hers. Judging from the fact her feet tangled with his calves and his wide chest enveloped her in solid heat, he was built tall, at least six feet, and like a wall of iron. While he didn't exactly pin her to the mattress, he made moving a challenge. Well, him and the handcuffs encircling her wrists.

She wasn't going anywhere, and he was making sure she understood that without a single word.

Fresh fear zipped up her spine. Holy cow, Mr. Mysterious hadn't failed to show up after all.

Be careful what you wish for...

Yeah, Lauren wished she'd thought in detail about the fact a stranger had vowed to strip her down and fill her up, rather than focusing simply on how nice it was to be noticed and wanted. This stranger had sneaked into her house, and he didn't have a rousing game of checkers on his mind. Oh, God. Would she wind up a police statistic?

"I can't wait to be inside you, to make you mine."

His deep, husky voice penetrated her panic and scratched her senses. Adrenaline jolted her. She opened her mouth to scream...but his hand still covered it.

Something about his words tore at her mind. *I can't wait to be inside you, to make you mine...* His voice sounded both menacing and seductive. Did he mean those words to be a promise or a threat?

Fear and thrill clawed at her belly. She couldn't separate them. Her mind spun, her heart pounded, and an icy slide of dread shocked her bloodstream. With the erection he pressed against her thigh, he felt fully prepared to do exactly what he'd stated and had beyond adequate equipment with which to do it. Way beyond.

For a flash of a second, she struggled. She should have told Noah she needed extra security. Should have called the police. God, how had this man stolen into her house? Handcuffed her to her own bed? Yes, she wanted excitement, but not the kind that meant she and her funeral arrangements would be the talk of the five o'clock news.

"Shh. You're going to scream. Long and loud. But not out of fear. I won't hurt you," he promised. "Ever. Just pleasure you."

With one hand over her mouth, the stranger placed the other on her shoulder and skimmed her flesh just beneath the strap of her camisole. Instead of tearing into her, he stroked her, his touch torturously unhurried. Lauren held her breath as his fingers moved across her skin, closer and closer to her breast.

What would he do? How would he touch her? It seemed unlikely he'd just seduce her and not hurt her. On the other hand, did the average serial killer have lingerie delivered to his victim's office first? No.

That realization only confused her more. She'd love to believe this was just a seduction. But why would he go to this much trouble just to get her into bed? She was hardly movie star gorgeous.

For some reason, he had gone to great lengths to get her beneath him—and doing a damn fine job with his opportunity—as he traced the swell of her breast, toyed with the hint of cleavage above the camisole. She held in a gasp.

Against her better judgment, tingles erupted. Her nipples peaked. Pleasure bubbled inside her, scraping against fear to create a totally new sensation. Jagged. Intense. Parts south suddenly gushed with moisture.

Oh, God. She was out of her mind. Her stomach coiled with fear and she got wet when he touched her. What was the matter with her?

Ashamed, afraid, aroused, Lauren trembled as his fingertips traced ever-smaller circles around her nipples. What should she do? Fight this stranger who'd invaded her home and promised to do the same to her body? Yes!

But his gentle invasion, his touch, sent frissons of excitement dancing across her skin, sugary sensations that pushed past her resistance and roused the dormant woman inside her. God, would it be too wrong to give in to the heat building inside her and let him have his way?

Before she could answer her question, he plucked at the ties, gave a little yank, and the garment opened, fell away. Lauren couldn't see, but the cool air caressing her nipples told her he'd bared them to his gaze. They tightened again. She held her breath, hoping he wouldn't touch them.

Hoping he would.

"I've got to see this. See you."

At her side, he shifted, leaned away, dropping his hand from her mouth. Then she heard the little click of the small light on her nightstand. Though she could see nothing behind her blindfold, she knew a muted golden light now suffused the room.

He curled his fingers around her breast and swiped a thumb across one of the peaks, groaning low and long. Lauren swallowed, her heart racing like a rollercoaster on a downhill run. He did it again. She bit her lip to hold in a moan.

The bed dipped beneath his full weight again, and he continued his attention to her breast, squeezing, rolling the hard tip between his fingers. "Gorgeous. I've imagined…"

His strained whisper scraped at her composure, her resistance. He burned her. Was she so desperate to be touched that a stranger who'd broken into her house and fondled her could turn her on? In a word, yes.

"Who are you?" The shaking in her voice was unmistakable.

"Shh. Later…"

"But—"

He transferred his attention to the other breast for a moment, plumping her flesh, stroking her nipple. Lauren's words died, forgotten, under an onslaught of sensation.

"Your breasts are gorgeous, rounder than they look in clothes."

"I sometimes wear a minimizer bra," she blurted.

"Don't. Ever again." His voice was like the lash of a whip. "You're too beautiful to hide."

Pleasure shot down her belly, centering…right where he'd need it if he intended to get inside her. And the way she felt now, she didn't think wetness was going to be a problem.

Was she insane? Was she actually contemplating having sex with a total stranger?

She couldn't. Shouldn't. It was crazy. Certifiable. Totally insane.

All true, yet…Lauren felt his exhalation brush her lips, like he hovered right above her. Like he was going to—

Before she could complete the thought, his mouth crashed over hers in a kiss that tore her breath—and every rational thought—away. Fear barely had time to flicker inside her before it was lost in the feel of his hot mouth sliding over hers, his strong hands tilting her head so he could find the perfect fit. He groaned deep from his chest.

Lauren gasped at the scalding shock of desire jolting her. And her stranger took advantage of her parted lips, stealing inside and thrusting deep. She tasted his hunger, his hot, wild demand. Pure desire went to her head faster than liquor.

The man could kiss. Make a woman feel utterly possessed with just his mouth.

He slid his hands beneath her in an urgent grip, pulling her under every hard, hot inch of him. Then those big hands grasped her thighs and pulled them apart. Lauren didn't even have the chance to draw a breath before he settled into the cradle of her thighs, as if he belonged there. Had every right to be there. With his muscled legs, he shoved her thighs wider.

Lauren opened her mouth. She really ought to protest. But another wild sweep of his tongue through her mouth and a rock of his hips that bumped his impressive cock right against her clit made her swallow her words. Against her better judgment—did she have any left?—pleasure arced through her, undeniable. Liquid heat doused her, drowning her protests. Senses spinning, her body ached with need.

He could soothe your ache. He could fulfill you.

As if sensing her inner struggle, he swept through her mouth again with possessive abandon. He coaxed her with the soft demand of his lips, the tangle of his tongue with hers, the taut cradle of his arms around her. Harsh...but holding back to show her he could be gentle, despite the hunger she sensed whipped him every moment they touched.

Lord knew it lashed her like a cat-o'-nine-tails on steroids.

Had she ever ached this badly? Wanted with such sudden intensity? Hell no. If Tim had been able to do this to her, she would have never let the man out of her sight.

"Want you," he breathed harshly in her ear. "So damn bad."

His words made her belly—and something a tad lower—pulse with a ferocious beat. Lauren stopped fighting the battle she couldn't hope to fight. He melted her. Completely. Made her dizzy. Crazy. She'd never known anything like it.

Moaning into his mouth, she arched up to him and kissed him. He answered with a groan, curling his tongue around hers, entangling them again. She invited him to take his fill. Surrendered.

The stranger didn't hesitate to take his possession deeper. He held her face in his hands gently, as if she were precious to him. But his kiss... He took her mouth again in a fierce mating, throbbing with harsh hunger. The flame of his desire ignited her even more. Lauren

37

felt every crush of his lips and lash of his tongue against her own deep inside her, where she was now soaking and aching and praying he would replace it all with satisfaction. Soon.

She fought the cuffs, wanting to touch him, feel the sleek, hard flesh she knew lurked under his soft cotton shirt. They jangled with finality. Arching, entreating, she whimpered into his mouth. On their own, her legs parted farther, wrapped around him.

"Yes," he growled. "Give me everything."

He rocked against her again, and the ache between her legs tightened. She was on fire now. God, the heat raged inside her, demanding she know the taste of his skin, the feel of his bunching shoulders under her palms as he thrust every inch of his cock inside her.

"Uncuff me," she panted against his chest. "Please."

"Next time."

He drew back, and she felt cold without him. Until she heard the rustling of clothing. He was undressing.

This was happening, really happening. A stranger was actually stripping in her bedroom with every intent to have sex with her. Lauren would have thought she was dreaming if it didn't feel so real.

"If you touch me now, I'll explode."

A whisper of misgiving shifted through her. "I'm afraid. I—I've never been tied down."

He leaned over her, and Lauren felt his heat seep inside her, the brush of his bare skin arousing. "Get used to it. I'm going to love having you bound and under me so I can watch you come while you're at my mercy."

Oh, God. He'd already stripped down to his skin. Now, he was stripping her of her defenses. His wicked words, coupled with the confession that he wanted her badly, tore away at her patience. But something tugged at her. Something familiar about his voice. Had she heard it somewhere?

A fast, fierce kiss put an end to the thought. His clever tongue swept through her mouth and captured hers. The kiss became a tango of shallow breaths and urgency, all fueled by his buttery-rich skill. He kissed her ruthlessly, like a man with just one thing on his mind.

He was making her think about sex, too. In fact, she couldn't think about anything else.

The cacophony of sensations ricocheted through her body, settling right where she ached like she'd been without sex for centuries, not a couple of years.

"Hurry," she demanded.

"I've waited so damn long. I'm not rushing this."

He'd waited? For her?

The puzzle made no sense, but his gruff whisper shot both a fresh thrill and a protest through her. Her body throbbed like a ceaseless toothache. He was going to make her wait.

"You've flushed the prettiest pink. Everything about you turns me on." His raspy whisper throbbed inside her.

His voice…low and rough and arousing. A hint of something familiar. Should she know it?

Lauren frowned, trying to puzzle it out with her overheated brain. But he settled on top of her again, her sensitive breasts meeting the hot slab of his chest. Think tank time was over.

A light dusting of hair grazed her nipples. And he was hard everywhere—pecs, abs, cock, thighs—all taut and ready and covering her with the intent to take. Electricity sparked every sensitive spot on her skin. Lauren softened around him, her body fitting against him perfectly, molding her every curve to his hard angles. Amazing. Like pieces of a puzzle made for each other. Perfect.

She raised her hip to him. "Now."

"I'm dying to." The words were a tortured moan. "But I have to get my mouth on you first. I have to taste you."

Before she could protest, his lips brushed the side of her breast. Heat curled everywhere he kissed and laved. He lifted his head, and Lauren swore she could *feel* his gaze on her nipples. More blood rushed to them, engorging them.

"Fucking beautiful," he murmured as his tongue curled around the sensitive tip.

Pleasure washed over her, cascading down her senses like a hot fall of liquid desire. She moaned, arched toward him—and he rewarded her by sucking her breast deep into his mouth. Voracious. His hard pulls tugged the ache between her legs into something sharp and impatient. A gentle scrape of his teeth, a subtle nip, then explosions of sensation detonated all through her, and she cried out.

"So responsive," he praised as he transferred his attention to her other nipple.

He laved it with the same care, a hard suck, a small stinging bite. The pleasure ratcheted up, the ache clamping down deep in her sex. She clenched her hands into fists. Perspiration filmed her chest. She couldn't breathe. Couldn't think.

Lauren could only want.

And when he smoothed his palm down her belly, yanked off her thong, and slid his hot finger through her aching wet slit, she cried out.

"Oh, hell," he panted against her breast. "You're bare. Do you shave?"

"Wax," she moaned.

"That's so damn sexy."

It was merely cleaner to her, but everything he did was sexy. Everything he said made her feel sexy. No one had made her feel like a desirable woman in a *very* long time. She wanted more. Now.

She opened her mouth to make a demand of her own when he circled his fingers around her swollen, humid opening, sensitizing her to his touch. Before she could take another breath, he plunged two fingers deep.

Oh, God. She was dissolving. Disintegrating. Coming apart already. How much of her mind would she lose if he thrust his cock inside her?

"I knew you'd feel amazing," he groaned.

But she barely heard. Pleasure ripped a cry from her throat. He was sending her into a spiral she had never experienced, had barely imagined in her wildest fantasies. And he thought *she* was amazing?

He twisted his fingers inside her and hooked them upward, reaching a sensitive spot in her slick channel that nearly had her coming off the bed. And if he kept touching her there, she'd be coming. Period.

Lauren thrust her hips up and pleaded, "Now. Please."

"Soon."

"But—"

As he thrust his fingers deep again, she felt him shake his head. No.

Damn!

Soft strands of his hair tickling her skin as he shifted down, his mouth leading the way. Pressing soft kisses on her shoulder, the side of her breast, her belly…lower, she gasped, writhed, moaned.

"I've got to taste you." The words were a harsh whisper against the bare flesh of her sex as he rubbed and pressed against the ultra-sensitive spot inside her. "Open for me, Lauren."

She did, probably setting a new world record as she bent her knees, raised to him in invitation. Ready, eager, for him to envelop her, fill her...fulfill her.

"You're damn tight," he gritted, maneuvering his fingers into the hot depths of her sex. "How long has it been?"

She was about to explode into a million pieces and he wanted her to answer a question? "Two years, " she gasped. "And a few months."

"Then let's make sure you're good and wet before I fuck you. Because I'm going to tonight. Hard."

Tim had never talked dirty. Never been edgy or blunt. For years, sex with him had been mechanical and automatic. Silent. Her stranger brought an intensity to the bedroom that drove her wild. Well, that and the way he touched her. The way he noticed her flushing skin, responded to her fresh waxing, cared about her part of the experience.

Whoever he was when he wasn't seducing her, he must be at least a somewhat decent guy.

If that was the case, why would he resort to sneaking into her house and cuffing her to her bed to get her attention?

Good question. And she really ought to get an answer now. Many answers, actually. Caving in to ruthless seduction by a breaking and entering seducer? Some rational part of her brain reasserted itself and insisted she wasn't ready to raise the white flag. Begging a stranger to claim her body and take her as he pleased? Stupid.

"Do I know you?"

"No questions. Not tonight."

"Yes, tonight. Right—"

He glided a thumb across her clit, the sweet, hot friction robbing her ability to speak.

"Ohmigod!"

"More?" he taunted.

No, get the hell out—of my body, my bed, my life; it should be the automatic response. It wasn't nearly as automatic as whimpering and lifting her hips to him.

She fought to whip up her defiance. But why fight everything she'd been wanting since her divorce? Hell, since her marriage to Tim had gone south? Lauren wanted passion, hot and wild with no strings attached. This stranger was giving it to her, as if he knew her body so intimately, so perfectly.

"Yes," she gasped.

"Good girl. I've got a reward for you…"

The fiery press of desire burned between her legs. His hot exhalations grazed her clit, sending her temperature spiking.

Before she could berate and beg him in the same breath, he settled his head between her legs, wiggled those fingers still impaling her, and ran the tip of his tongue right over her clit.

Lauren screamed with the livewire sensation. Shocking hot. Wickedly destructive.

The sensations magnified when he sucked her clit into his mouth. The wet blade of his tongue stroked her sensitive nubbin, shredding her self-control.

With a loud cry, Lauren arched to him, gripping the headboard in her fists.

"That's it," he urged. "I've thought about doing this to you so many times…" he murmured against her slick folds.

Shelley Bradley

In an insistent pace, he kissed, nipped, suckled, thrust—and utterly possessed her. Pleasure soared. Blood engorged her flesh, making every swipe of his tongue even more sensitive than the last. Her heart roared like a wild gong in her ears. *Boom, boom, boom.* Tighter, tighter, the ache coiled, building into something beyond big. Huge was too small. Gigantic. Phenomenal. Mind-bending.

"Oh! Oh my…" she panted.

"Now," he demanded, thrusting his fingers into her depths and finding just the right spot as another lash from his tongue had her ache peaking, her pleasure skyrocketing.

With a scream, she exploded in a never-ending series of spasms and clamped down on his fingers, ecstasy saturating her.

Lauren had barely caught her breath before the stranger wound his way up her body, covering her. Every inch of his body was rigid with hunger, taut with holding back. She shivered, knowing what he'd want next.

Feeling how much she wanted it, too.

"Are you still on the pill?"

Still? He knew she had been? Did he know about her irregular periods, too? "Yes."

"Good. Got to fuck you. Now," he growled. "Nothing between us."

"Nothing?" She panicked. No condom?

"I'm healthy. I promise."

"I can't just take the word of a stranger." Even if he sounded so damn sincere.

"I swear, I haven't touched a woman without a condom in twenty years. I just had a physical, and I'm clean. You're safe. I would never endanger you in any way. Please." His grip tightened on her. "Please."

44

Odd and crazy, but she believed him. Or maybe she was just melting from the inside out at the idea of nothing between them but more of the passion he was so adept at giving in a world-class way. Whatever it was, she did one of the most wild, impulsive things of her life and gave him a shaky nod, her chest rising, falling, aching.

Hell, she'd just come as well as any porn star, but his intensity and determination alone were enough to renew her arousal.

He fitted his hands beneath her, then cupped her ass in the hot scald of his hands, and whispered, "I'm going to get inside you, so damn deep you won't remember what it's like without me there. I'm going to make you ache, make you beg. Make you mine."

ལ ལ ལ

Noah took a deep breath, determination to do exactly as he said washing through him. And by the time tonight was over, she was going to feel his possession all the way down to her heart.

Under the soft golden light beside her bed, she flushed a pretty pink once more and bit her lip, now swollen from his kisses. Her soft blondish-brown curls tumbled around her shoulders, longer strands caressing the pale column of her neck and curling toward her breasts.

God, she was gorgeous. And he couldn't believe that tonight— finally—she was his.

A fact that wasn't going to change—not if he could help it.

Lauren Southall was about to experience what ten years of a man's pent-up lust felt like.

Hell, he'd tried everything—every woman—to take away the edge. He'd known for years, from the first time he met Lauren, shook her hand, and saw those brown eyes dancing with life and humor, that he *had* to have her. But Tim's wife had been off-limits. Over the years, he'd seen her happiness dim, known the divorce was inevitable. And he'd bided his time, occupying it with women like Misty who expected nothing more than good sex and a nice parting gift.

Now, his waiting and planning—the biting ache for a woman he could see and talk to, laugh with and touch casually, but never *have*— was all about to be over.

Noah swallowed hard, gripped her hip with one hand and guided himself to her steamy entrance with the other. He eased in an inch, gritting his teeth against the hot silk of her wet sheath tightening on him, still rippling with gentle aftershocks.

The blindfold shielded her eyes from him, and he cursed the necessity of protecting his identity so she could feel him—and not be weirded out by the fact she was fucking Tim's buddy and her boss. But damn, he wanted to see her expressive eyes widen as he filled her.

He would, he promised himself. Someday, he'd look right into those saucy dark eyes as he gave her every inch he had, every bit of love he'd been feeling for years. First, he had to own her body, prove he could master it. Surely, her heart and her body were connected, so once he'd conquered one, the other couldn't be too far behind.

The claiming was going to start—and end—tonight.

She gasped at the feel of him breaching her, and he watched a sweet flush creep down her cheeks, between her collarbones. Already she was scalding him. Killing him with her heat. What a way to go...

He covered her lips with his own, penetrating her mouth as he pushed his way inside her body, inch by torturous inch. Under him, Lauren moaned, her sex clamping down on his cock, her heels in the small of his back.

Slick. A smooth glide. Down, down. He tunneled into her in a seemingly endless stroke until he was finally seated to the hilt. God, she was tight. Silken. Better than any woman in memory. Better than any fantasy.

He groaned, throwing his head back as she took him completely, the head of his cock pushing against her womb.

"Oh, that feels good." Her voice fluttered.

Understatement of a fucking lifetime. Especially when she tilted her hips up to him and he slid in another half inch. Even his testicles rested tight against her now. He'd never felt anything like the electric pleasure pulsing through him.

Noah took a deep breath. "Hang on."

She sent him a shaky nod. And he pulled back, back until just a fraction of his head remained inside her, then he drove deep again. Lauren cried out. The sharp note echoed through the room, throwing a shiver down his spine. And she closed around him, her body sucking him back in, clinging.

Jesus, two strokes into this, and she was already blowing his mind. He had no doubt a third would feel every bit as good.

Better, Noah soon found out. Pleasure shot up his cock, coiling heat low in his belly, curling his toes.

On the fourth stroke, he invaded her mouth again, mimicking the action of their bodies with their tongues. Lauren melted around him, opening, accepting, smelling so damn good. And meeting him with every downward stroke, tipping up to him, ripping through his control.

But he couldn't stop, even though he felt like he was driving a hundred miles an hour down a twisting road while blindfolded. He was destined to crash. Hard. But in this case, it would be so damn worth it.

Not until Lauren crashed with him, however.

Bracing his hands against her hips, Noah forced himself to slow down. Deliver each thrust with deliberate impact and maximum friction. Gritting his teeth, he growled as he filled her to the hilt again. Beneath him, Lauren's little pants as she tried to catch her breath were driving him out of his mind.

As he found her magic little spot, the one guaranteed to fast forward her into orgasm, she writhed.

With short digs of his cock, he worked the spot, dragging the head, which felt as if it had ballooned ten times its normal size, right where she needed it. She rewarded him quickly, breath catching, flush spreading across her fair skin, thighs latching on, pussy tightening.

"I—oh! Help. I need…"

"I know what you need," he rasped into her ear. "I'm going to give it to you."

He did. He lengthened his strokes again to deliver friction, rub her G-spot, then nudge her clit with his pelvis at the end.

"Yes," she cried out.

He did it again and again, thrusting deep, jolting her cervix with every fierce downward stroke until her vaginal walls fisted him and rippled with the pending explosion. Balls deep, he rocked against her again.

"Yes." Her fists gripped the headboard. "Yes!"

One more long, calculated plunge inside her and she came apart.

So did his self-control.

The feel of her squeezing him, milking his cock as she screamed and grabbed the bed posts…too much for his overwrought body. He needed her too much. Needed to mark her somehow. It was crazy and primitive and he'd never felt such an urge in his life, but Noah wasn't about to deny it, not when white fire shot up the length of his erection, starbursting ecstasy through his body as he shouted in satisfaction and came deep inside her fluttering pussy.

Slowly they caught their breath. A minute slid by. Another. Noah didn't resist the urge to kiss her cheeks, the tip of her pert nose, her swollen mouth. He caressed the line from her hip to her waist until he wandered up to her breast, settling over her shoulder. He held her close. And didn't move.

He could stay like this, with her, forever.

Being with Lauren was…beyond anything he'd ever known. He wanted to grab her, blurt everything, especially his love. Then make love to her again.

But she lay under him, growing still and tense. Unease skittered down his spine, disturbing his perfect bliss. *Damn*, he thought as she unhooked her legs from about his waist. Even though his half-hard dick was still inside her, he could almost feel her pulling away physically. Emotionally.

Why?

"Who are you?"

Before coming here, he'd planned to make love to her, then reveal his identity. Let her deal with it so they could start having sex, start sharing their hearts. But now…his gut was telling him it wasn't going to be that simple.

What if taking her to bed once wasn't enough to erase her qualms about getting involved with him? What if she still saw just Noah Reeves, boss, buddy and all-around good guy? He could practically feel her shoving her defenses back into place.

He had a bad feeling it was going to take more than one tango between the sheets to make her body his.

"Who are you?" she demanded again. "I could swear I know your voice…"

He hesitated, his insides clenching as he tried to listen to his gut. It told him revealing all now would not help his cause. At all. It also chided him to try even harder to disguise his voice.

"Later," he whispered, moving in to kiss her again.

She tore her mouth away. "Now."

He heard the panic in her voice and held in a curse. "Shh."

"No, I won't shush. I can't believe I just—just…"

"Made love with a stranger?"

"Did I? I can't make love with someone I don't know."

"You know me," he admitted quietly, careful to disguise his voice. "But you don't know *me*. You don't see me."

"Let me see you now."

Noah hesitated. She had perfectly valid points. Good ones, even. But she wasn't ready. If she turned away now, he'd never get another chance. Lauren could be frighteningly closed and private when it suited her. She'd shut him out completely.

He wasn't about to let her go.

"Didn't you like it?"

Between her forehead and the set of her mouth, Noah knew she would have given him an incredulous stare if she could have. "Like it? I don't think I've ever climaxed so hard in my life. You're good. Obviously. But you…took me."

"Yeah, and I'm going to do it again. But make no mistake, I made love to you, too," he protested gruffly.

Damn, it was hard to change his voice every time he opened his mouth, especially with his mind racing. He wished he could just talk to her as himself, rip off her blindfold, show her who he was, tell her what he felt. Figure out why she was resisting the idea of making love.

But she wasn't ready to deal with any of what he wanted.

Lauren shook her head. "No."

"You want it softer and sweeter, so you know I'm making love to you?"

"No."

Now she sounded positively panicked. Noah frowned.

"You just want sex? Wham, bam, thank you, ma'am?"

She hesitated, drew in a ragged breath, and sent him a shaky nod.

He froze as a suspicion took shape in his mind. Was Lauren against having a man in her life for anything more than sex? Against love? If so, he didn't need a PhD to know her divorce had to be the cause. She'd never acted bitter. Sure, she'd been sad, reserved for a while, but resolved to move on with life. Her rejection of love surprised him. Was she scared? Of loss? Of more pain? He'd get to the bottom of the issue...just as soon as he made a point.

"I want more," he murmured against her neck. "I want to love you. Right now."

‹З ‹З ‹З

The stranger's sandpaper whisper reverberated in Lauren's belly, rattling her self control.

No love. Absolutely not. Love didn't last. Love hurt when the relationship was over. Ali McGraw had been really wrong when she said love meant never having to say you're sorry. Lauren had apologized to Tim for everything she could think of...but in the end, she'd known his heart had left her in favor of a shiny new job, another promotion, trips to far-flung places. Men weren't built for lasting love.

She hated the broken hearts and dreams left behind.

This man above her, still buried balls deep, would be no different. He might want her now, but his desire wouldn't last. Neither would his "love".

But his skill with her body, the way he could make her flush with a word and ache with a mere kiss…all dangerous—to her self control, to her psyche. Even to her heart, since he could use her body to get to her emotions. And when the game was over and the challenge was gone, where would she be?

Alone and broken hearted. No thanks.

Lauren tensed, squirmed under him, wriggling her hips to dislodge him from her sex.

The friction of his cock rubbed the sensitive inner walls, igniting flickers of sensations. She gasped. Those flickers turned to sparks when he moved against her, bumping her clit, creating more delicious friction. Inside her, she felt him engorge. He grew thick, long, until he occupied every part of her sex again, pushing all the way against her cervix. So hard, as if he hadn't come at all. As if he was completely prepared to go full throttle again.

But he didn't. Instead, he stunned her with a leisurely withdrawal, easing out one torturously slow inch at a time. The head of his cock scraped against her slick flesh with every breath.

He touched his mouth to hers. A soft brush of lips, a tangle of sighs. With a firm, gentle stroke of his mouth, he urged her lips wider, tempting her to accept him deep. Lauren didn't have the will to stop him, and he didn't waste time before possessing her mouth in a velvety wet embrace. His tongue lazed its way inside, catching her own. The kiss was so unabashedly intimate it made her toes curl. It compelled her to respond, flooded her with not just heat, but warmth.

With a helpless ache, she writhed under him as he eased back inside her, and she squeezed his cock with her sheath. Sensations tore past her awareness and buzzed in her brain.

Oh my God.

He ripped his mouth away and moaned against her neck, into her ear. The sound sent flashes of pleasure dancing down her spine. His five o'clock shadow rasped against her jaw. And his hands... *Help me now!* Those hands of his swept down from her shoulders, lightly tracing her collarbones before caressing straight to her breasts. Despite her mammoth orgasm a few short minutes ago, Lauren felt the blood rush to her nipples. They stood up and welcomed his fingers, which accepted the invitation immediately and toyed with the sensitive tips.

Gentle, teasing strokes over the hard points. Unhurried. Like he wanted to learn her, find out exactly what pleased her. The warmth from his fingers as he brushed and plucked at her nipples became heat. The ache seeped past her defenses and multiplied.

Even as he withdrew again nearly all the way, he touched her like she was fragile and precious. A soft sweep of fingers here, a tender caress of his lips there. Her body swelled under every touch. But what she felt was more. Much more. The longing to touch and be touched had been there, but now a desperation to matter to someone—to this man—swathed her in sweet longing.

No. This couldn't be happening. Her body was hers to control, not his to play at will. Unfortunately, her body didn't exactly agree with her logic. And if she wasn't careful, she feared her heart wouldn't be far behind.

Her breasts swelled for his touch, the sensitive areolas bunched up around nipples so needy that when he bent his head to take one of the hard beads in his mouth, she gasped. And arched to him.

He accepted her offering, and a warm burst of emotion broke free in her chest. She couldn't wrap her arms around him, so she hugged him with her legs, keeping him close.

Violently aware of the head of his cock barely tucked inside her sex and the throb of her desire pounding at her, Lauren raised her hips to entice this stranger to bury himself deep inside her again.

She didn't just want the man. She *needed* him.

The pleasure of his hot lips over her, the deft curl of his tongue against her, had her moaning. The soft, insistent pull of his mouth at her nipple quickly reduced her to a whimper. She could feel her sex clenching, silently begging. Lauren struggled against the cuffs again. She wanted to put her hands on him, sink her fingers into his hair, then move lower to feel the muscles of his back work as he thrust into her. The idea of grabbing him and pulling him back inside her so he could fill her again amplified her need.

She had this wonderful, terrible feeling that with him buried deep within her, she'd feel complete.

Already, the peak of desire rose. Her breathing shallowed. Of their own volition, her thighs parted wider and she raised her hips. Still, he held himself away, kept her on a torture rack as she waited, panting with unfulfilled desire. He switched his attention to her other nipple, plucking it with his lips, nipping gently with his teeth while his hands drifted down her body to clench around her hips.

Without warning, he buried his face in her neck and inched into her. Slowly. So damn slowly, Lauren was sure she was going to lose her mind. When he had an inch inside her, her heartbeat pounded in her ears, roaring out all thoughts. In two inches, and she grabbed the headboard and moaned. In halfway now. Something soft and dangerous expanded in her chest. Damn, he was killing her with his slow pleasure. Hyping up nerves that hadn't seen action since the Clinton Administration, shutting down normal logic. In six inches, and he was still moving forward at that relentlessly unhurried pace. She thrashed her head from side to side as the desire racing through her blood turned from hot to scalding and the need to feel him everywhere overcame her. Finally, he was in those last few inches, pressing against the mouth of her cervix, bumping her clit. Somehow breaking down barriers to her emotions.

She screamed, then started gasping for breath.

"I'm going to love you like this every chance I get," he muttered roughly in her ear.

Before she could say no—or say anything—her body rejoiced.

He repeated the whole process of agonizing withdrawal, followed by an endless, tormenting thrust inside her. And all the while, his fingers and mouth toyed with nipples that stood so straight, he had to know they were saluting a job well done.

The friction alone set her on fire, but when he added a little bump and grind at the end, her clit throbbed, pulsed, swelled. She placed an open-mouthed kiss on his bare shoulder and tasted hot male and sweat and desire on her tongue. Her pulse careened out of control. Emotions were a cacophony of words and needs all bouncing within her, dying to burst free. Sweat covered her as he repeated his slow-motion stroke a third time, then a fourth.

God help her, she wasn't going to last a fifth.

But she had to try.

Lauren bit her lip and tried to take her mind elsewhere. Hockey games, Emma needing stitches after falling on a sprinkler head, really boring meetings.

During which she usually sat across from Noah and found ways to stare at him while pretending not to. She imagined Noah tunneling into her right now, those stunning eyes of his hot with passion as he gripped her hips, held her still for his invading cock and sent her on a slow path to insanity. To ecstasy, as he whispered that he wanted to love her every chance he got.

Lauren's pleasure ramped up in a millisecond. Now beyond her control, her arousal climbed, soared, until it twisted her belly in a tense knot. On another downward stroke of his slow, insistent cock, she exploded, squeezing down on his erection so hard, he couldn't move inside her. He pulsed, then spilled his hot seed. His tormented groan ripped through the night, joining her sharp cry.

Tears singed the backs of her eyes as he wrapped his arms around her and held her against his body, as if he'd never touched anything more important. As if nothing would ever be more important than what they shared.

An illusion, a mirage. Not true. Means nothing. She chanted it all in her mind as the pleasure ebbed slowly. She wasn't sure she believed it. Sex with someone who refused to tell her even his name couldn't actually mean anything, right?

In a normal world, yes. Lauren got the feeling she wasn't in Kansas anymore, at least where this man was concerned.

The silence overcame the room quickly, punctuated only by his harsh breaths. And her shuddering cries as she tried to keep her tears at bay. She didn't succeed.

Mr. Mysterious had completely taken control of her body in a slow, thorough imitation of real lovemaking. It couldn't be real. But...how the hell had he torn a gaping hole in her defenses so quickly? Worse, thoughts of Noah hadn't just aroused her or sent her over the edge, they'd ripped her emotions wide open.

She didn't understand this. The horrified knowledge of the melting ice around her heart scared her to death. She felt open and raw and vulnerable in a way she didn't think she'd ever been.

"Get out," she rasped.

"What?" His arms tightened around her. "Lauren—"

"Go."

Tears seeped down her cheeks, and he wiped them away with a tender caress of his thumbs. "Are you hurt?"

"Don't act like you care. This was sex. Just sex. You've had it. Now get the hell out!"

"Just sex?" he growled, his voice finally rising above a whisper.

Something familiar about his voice tugged at her, but she was discombobulated and strung out on a flood of feeling she'd been holding back for too long.

"Yes," she hurled back at him defiantly.

"Why are you crying?"

"Because I let a total stranger fuck me. Twice."

He went taut above her. Anxiety shot through her. She'd pissed him off. His body language shouted his anger. What would he do? Lauren didn't think he'd harm her. He wasn't crazy or violent. If nothing else, she'd felt his essence, harsh when necessary, giving when he could be, while he was deep inside her.

But she hated the thought that she'd hurt his feelings.

Damn, why the hell did she care about how he felt? Unless she cared, too...

Not a good development.

"I made love to you, and you know it. For a minute there, you made love back to me."

"No," she choked.

"Yes, and you'll do it again."

"Never."

He withdrew and eased off the bed. From the sounds of his rustling clothes, he dressed quickly. Suddenly he secured her wrists to the headboard loosely with something else, something soft and pliable. Velvet ropes? He unhooked the cuffs.

"By the time you work these ties free and remove the blindfold, I'll be gone. But I'll be back." He pressed a quick kiss to her mouth, and she breathed in a lungful of hot-male and sex-scented air. "And when I return, I'm going to make you eat those words."

Chapter Four

Monday started bright and early with an eight a.m. meeting Lauren had been anticipating for weeks. The restaurant chain's expansion into the affluent areas north and west of Dallas was one of her projects. Noah had given her a lot of latitude in choosing sites and tweaking the menu to suit the locations. Today, she'd present her recommendations to Noah and the rest of the committee and, with approval, they'd get started on focus groups that would assist them in making the suburban offering just right.

Today, she struggled to dredge up her normal enthusiasm.

Staring into a cup of black sludge the mini-mart around the corner from her house passed off as coffee, Lauren sloughed off the thought that she needed to be gathering her papers and making her way to the conference room. Instead, her stubborn mind was still fixated on Friday night.

Every time she thought back on that magical, frightening encounter, she flushed and heated. The man had known her body. How to control it. How to please her. Better, even, than she'd known. He'd understood exactly how to take her higher, precisely how to cast her over the edge. He'd done it with ruthless skill.

He'd also stolen past her defenses and made love to her.

How?

Despite her brave words to Noah last Friday afternoon, she wasn't a casual sex sort of girl. Oh, the idea had appeal. All the pleasure, none of the strings that eventually brought pain when the relationship died and someone left… But deep down, she was the kind of girl whose body followed her heart. Her Friday night stranger had given her a fabulous handful of orgasms, true—but she couldn't escape her good-girl roots. She'd allowed—oh, let's be honest—begged a man whose name she didn't even know to invade her sex…and he'd slipped into her soul. And she'd responded with abandon. Lauren had never given herself that completely to any man, not even her husband of nearly ten years.

Why?

It could only be because she'd been thinking of Noah. Somehow, someway, that man had gotten under her skin and chiseled his way into her heart.

But even before the naughty fantasies of her boss, she'd been responding to Mr. Mysterious with complete abandon, and the realization left her with part thrill…part shame. Had she changed? Did her body recognize her stranger as her ultimate sexual mate?

Or was it because something about the stranger tugged at her, and in her memories, he was enough like Noah to make her respond?

And to top it all off, rather than being glad she'd verbally chased him out of her bed after "the deed," she was sulky. He said he'd be back. Two whole days at home with the phone constantly near as she'd laid bathroom tile. *Nada.* Her girls had called. Tim had phoned to arrange a drop-off for the kids. Her mother had called to ask if she planned to come to Aunt Frannie's birthday party in two weeks.

She'd listened to every sound in the house, thinking he might sneak back in. Other than the postman delivering some clothes she'd bought the girls out of a catalog, no one else had come knocking.

Damn.

Mr. Mysterious had disappeared as completely and thoroughly as he had pleasured her.

To make matters worse, she tried to figure out who he was—and only got a headache for her efforts. Someone she knew, he'd said. She'd love for him to be Noah...but she knew better. He wasn't Gary in Accounting. Gary wasn't tall enough to be her stranger. Not Tim. She'd know her ex anywhere. Besides, she'd never responded to Tim like that, and he wasn't nearly as imaginative as Mr. Mysterious in bed. Who, then? A neighbor she hadn't noticed? Someone who worked in this building? None of those men knew her well. Certainly not well enough to know she was on the pill. Nothing added up.

"Good morning," a dark male voice rasped behind her, right in her ear.

She shivered. Noah. Had to be. But his voice with that husky note... It reminded her of her stranger.

Wishful thinking, girl. Stop now.

Lauren shot a sharp gaze up to him. Mistake. Big mistake. Pale blue eyes sparked with energy and something she couldn't define. A five o'clock shadow, despite the early hour, dark hair slightly mussed and spiked, and a killer suit that hugged his body every bit as tightly as she wanted to.

Pathetic. She really had to stop mooning over her boss. Over Tim's pal. God, if he knew the thoughts running through her head, he'd most likely laugh. If Noah knew how she'd responded to a stranger just by fantasizing about *him*, he would run for the hills.

Giving herself a mental shake, Lauren tried to clear her head. Noah sneaking into her house, cuffing her, stripping her naked, and rocking her world? In her dreams. But since she lived in reality, she knew better. *If* Noah was interested—big if—he'd simply ask her out on a nice, polite date. Dinner and a movie. A trip to an art gallery. The symphony. He wouldn't play Conan the Seducer. She'd seen him with enough women over the years to know it wasn't his style.

Through sheer appeal, he'd simply leave her breathless and wanting and saying yes. She liked him—too much. And it had to stop. Even if he started a fling with her—an even bigger if—he'd leave her, as he left every other woman. It would hurt like hell. Not to mention the fact her rapport with a longtime friend and her boss would be strained, to say the least.

More's the pity. She adored everything about him...including the smile he was flashing her way now.

"Morning," she answered.

"You ready?"

"Ready?" *For you to notice I'm female? I wish.*

"For this morning's meeting."

Of course. Business. *Keep your mind on business, girl.*

She nodded. "As I'll ever be. Your help with the prep last week really made the presentation stronger. You really are the master strategist. Thanks for your help."

"I think your plan is a solid one. Now it's up to you to convince the others. Speaking of which, shouldn't we be on our way to the room to set up?"

Lauren glanced at her watch—and nearly flinched. "Ten til eight? Oh, wow. Yeah."

Grabbing a stack of papers, she reached for the laptop with her presentation all loaded on the hard drive. Noah already had it in the grip of his large hand.

"I can get that."

He shrugged. "I know, but this frees you up to pour us fresh cups of coffee and take them to the meeting."

"True." She laughed. "You're always planning ahead."

"Always."

The firm emphasis on the word, coupled with a pointed glance, earned him a puzzled frown. What the heck was he up to?

"I need the caffeine desperately," he added. "Kind of a sleepless weekend. How about you?"

His answer put images in her had of Noah and Misty together, playing with her pom-poms...among other things. A bolt of something dark and painful pierced her gut. Lauren looked away, pretending to glance around to make sure she had everything. Once she was positive she had her act together and her expression under control, she hustled away from her desk. Noah fell into step beside her.

"I got the bathroom tile finished. Now I just have to seal the grout, but the girls can help me. They came home on Sunday night. Yesterday afternoon, Tim took them miniature golfing. Cassie loved it; Emma hated it. Typical."

"Emma doesn't like many activities that don't involve a book."

"Yep. And Cass only likes playing if she can get sweaty. They're very different."

"They're great girls, and I know you're proud."

"I am."

They reached the coffee bar, and Lauren poured them each a tall cup into waiting Styrofoam.

"Black, right?" she turned to Noah.

He jerked his gaze up to her face quickly then looked away, nodding. Had he been staring at her breasts? No. Not possible. But then…what *had* he been looking at?

Brushing the question off and scolding herself that she needed to get over this crazy infatuation, she added some artificial sweetener and creamer to her coffee and headed down the hall. Noah followed.

"What else did you do this weekend?" he asked. "Did Mr. Mysterious show up and make good on his promises?"

She was *not* answering him, even though she felt his ardent gaze glued to her profile. She was not going to tell Noah that a total stranger had snuck into her house and she had been waiting for him in red lace. She refused to admit aloud that he'd cuffed her to her bed and mastered her body in stunning ways she couldn't begin to describe. She would not say a word about the fact he'd used his tongue on every part of her body. Or the mind-melting kisses. Forget blabbing about the way he'd teased her clit until she'd exploded. She was not going to mention his huge erection filling every bit of her sex or confess he'd known the perfect stroke for maximum friction and killer orgasms. She'd never divulge how totally she'd given herself to him and cried afterward. Nope. Not a word. No way, no how.

"I'm guessing from the blush on your face the answer is yes." His grin widened to something mischievous and suggestive. "And I'll go out on a limb and guess that you liked it."

This was when she hated being fair skinned. Hard to keep secrets when a blush she couldn't control told pretty much the whole story.

"Who do I need to watch out for this morning? Who is going to push back the most during this meeting?" Maybe he'd take the old bait and switch. She hoped.

Noah just laughed. "You enjoyed it, didn't you? Whatever he did, it did the trick. You look surprisingly...relaxed this morning."

Silence. Lauren would rather cut out her tongue and eat it than admit to the man she had a major crush on that she'd surrendered her body to another man, a total stranger, while thinking of him.

But her confirmation or denial wouldn't change facts. Noah knew, at the minimum, that she'd given in and liked it. Apparently, the thought of another man in her bed didn't bother him. In the least.

Didn't that speak volumes about how much he didn't think about her sexually? Of how much he didn't want her? And why should he when he had Misty, who could no doubt cheer at the top of her lungs while doing the splits over his cock?

Her gut clenched. Her mood dropped lower than her knees.

"Not talking, huh?"

His cat-ate-the-canary grin crawled on her last nerve and squashed it. Hell, could he get any more obvious about the fact he was glad someone had screwed her? Not by much. Clearly it hadn't crossed his mind to wish he'd been the one doing the screwing.

"Noah, I didn't ask you about your weekend with Misty. Why are you asking me about mine with this guy?"

He tensed, frowned. "I didn't see Misty this weekend."

"What? Did she have an away game she had to cheer for?" Lauren couldn't stop a snide tone from creeping in.

"Something like that. I'm living vicariously through you. Spill the details."

Men. If he had drawn her a picture, he couldn't have been any clearer about the fact he was only interested in a second-hand thrill. "You're my boss, and this is an inappropriate conversation in general, much less five minutes before a very important meeting."

His smile fell. "Oh, sure. Sorry. I—I just want to see you happy. You looked... Did he make you happy?"

Lauren closed her eyes. Be short, sweet, and honest. She'd learned that was always the best way to deal with Noah. "Yes and no. I don't know him. He doesn't—"

"You don't know who he is? Still?"

He didn't sound surprised exactly. But the question in his tone suggested he was.

"No. He never said his name. I...couldn't see." God, she could feel a fresh flush spreading across her cheeks. "Anyway, he doesn't really know me. I have no idea why he picked me. He said he'd be back and he didn't show. I'm guessing it's over, and that's the end."

Finally, they reached the double doors to the meeting room. Through the glass, Lauren saw a couple of people already gathered inside. Thank God, this crazy, uncomfortable, disheartening conversation was going to end. And maybe for a few hours she could pretend that the man she wanted most wasn't amused by the fact another man spent Friday night in her bed.

After the meeting, she could go to the bathroom and kick a stall door or something to purge the fury and frustration churning her blood now.

Except Noah grabbed her arm, preventing her from heading into the conference room.

"I think you're underestimating this guy, sugar. And your appeal. He sounds like a man on a mission, and you're a beautiful woman. Don't be surprised if you see him again soon."

She shook her head. "I told him to leave."

Noah leaned in, his heat enveloping her, his very height and breadth making her feel small and feminine and lightheaded.

Dangerous things fluttered in her belly. Even more dangerous ideas rolled around in her mind.

"If he got half the welcome I suspect he did, then he knows you're not immune. He'll be back."

ର ର ର

Lauren's expression swam with annoyance as she walked past him into the conference room. Damn!

Okay, so asking her about Friday night right before the biggest meeting of her new career had been a bad idea. This morning's conversation, while ill-timed, certainly proved that Lauren had enjoyed Friday night. He'd known it, really. The feel of her pussy rippling around his cock and her screaming ringing in his ears told him that.

Noah blamed his blabbing of questions on his impatience. He was hooked on Lauren. Totally addicted. Forcing himself to stay away Saturday and Sunday, rather than returning and spending the weekend deep inside her, had been damn difficult. But he'd planned a new strategy after their less-than-satisfying parting had left him hungry and very clear that the battle for her heart, not her body, would be the far bigger challenge. He'd been so damn driven that he'd stayed up til all hours devising a better strategy. He had the perfect one now.

Mr. Mysterious would continue breaking down the barriers around Lauren's body. Noah himself would start seducing her heart— gently. She'd fall into the arms of both, he'd tell her they were one and the same, then all would be well. He hoped.

Her behavior after their lovemaking had been a shock. She didn't believe in happily ever after anymore? Didn't want love? Bullshit. Lauren was a happily-ever-after, white-picket-fence sort of woman.

This morning had been troubling, too. Lauren considered him a pal of sorts. Given that, why had she all but refused to tell him her perspective on Friday night? Then thrown Misty in his face? He'd stopped seeing the cheerleader a few weeks ago. Misty had lots between the waist and shoulders...not much north. Certainly not enough to interest him for more than a few hours.

And Lauren had acted almost...jealous. The thought made him grin.

Lauren tapped him on the shoulder, and Noah turned. She was right there, right in front of him. A sheer gloss sheened those full rosy lips, and the taste of her kiss was right on his tongue. He wanted it again. Now. He clenched his fists to keep his hands to himself. Not only was this not the right place, but it wasn't the right time. Lauren just wasn't ready. After she fell further under the spell of Mr. Mysterious...and Noah had edged her into the dreaded "R" word, *relationship*, then she'd be ready to handle the emotional stuff. He'd be patient about springing the "M" word on her. Or try to be.

"Can you hand me the laptop?" she asked, all business.

Noah frowned but complied, reaching behind him to grab it off the table. He watched as she opened the case and began setting up with quick movements. Without thought, he handed her cords and the box light as she needed them.

"Handouts?" he asked.

"End pouch."

He withdrew them, setting them in front of her. "You ready?"

Lauren swallowed, then nodded. She looked a bit nervous, but more resolute. And damn sexy, despite her professional navy blue suit and upswept hair.

"You'll do great," he whispered. "Martin is going to give you a hard time. Watch him. Don't lose your temper. Stay logical. You can win him over with cold, hard facts. You're smarter than him."

At his words, her gaze zipped up from the laptop right to his face. A moment of vulnerability crossed her face, and he wanted to take her in his arms so badly. Tim was his buddy, but he'd been a prick where his ex-wife was concerned. Noah knew the ass-wipe had done a number on her self-esteem.

Thanking God everyone else in the room seemed engrossed in their own conversations, he whispered, "I know Tim didn't treat you with the respect your intelligence deserves—"

She laughed. "Tim treated me like a cross between Airhead Barbie and the invisible woman. He could have cared less about my abilities beyond cooking and housekeeping."

"Tim can be an utter moron."

"Thank you." Her expression softened, and her gaze seemed to reach for him, linger. "On that, we're agreed."

"I'll help you today as much as I can. It's a good idea and an excellent plan. You know I'm on your side."

Her big brown eyes softened even more. "Thanks again. I know you've neglected your own projects to help me with this one. I appreciate you taking the time."

He shot her a direct stare. A heated one. Could she see it? Did she understand?

Lauren's gaze clung to him from beneath thick lashes before skittering away.

"Sugar," he whispered.

Her dark brown stare was back, uncertain, almost questioning.

"I'll always make time for you. Always."

Noah knew time—and Tim's amount of it away from Lauren and home—had been a centerpiece in the divorce. After their split, Tim had shown up at his place, shitfaced, and spilled his guts. Sensing his chance with Lauren after all these years, Noah hadn't stopped Tim's verbal regurgitation of their marital problems. Even Tim admitted he did everything he could to climb the corporate ladder and volunteered to travel whenever the subject came up. He had nothing against Lauren or marriage...but he didn't want either. Neither of them had cheated or lied. Tim had just acted as if Lauren and the girls didn't exist.

The guard in Lauren's gaze dropped, and suddenly he could see pain and...was he actually seeing longing?

"Hey, you two whispering the secrets of the universe, or are you going to start this meeting?" Gus Martin, one of Noah's partners, groused. "I've got other things to do this morning."

The jackass hadn't even finished speaking before Lauren's face closed up. She jerked away as if she was on fire and began straightening papers again. Noah resisted the urge to march across the room, grab Martin by the throat, and pound his head into a wall.

She stared right at her nemesis, giving him a cool, take-no-prisoners stare. Noah was so proud of her moxie and smarts, he nearly burst with it.

"I'm ready, Mr. Martin."

Chapter Five

"I think we did it!" Lauren shrieked the minute they entered Noah's office and he closed the door behind them.

"You did it," he corrected. "And I think you're right. The decision will come quickly and be favorable because you did great and kept your cool. You had all the right information. You gave Martin logical arguments. You shut him down when he tried to run you over. Everyone was impressed." He smiled.

Lauren basked in the glow. His eyes were a wintery blue, but that grin of approval made his whole expression so toasty, she could have roasted marshmallows by it. "I couldn't have done it without you. You're the one who made me ruthlessly prepare."

He stepped closer and shrugged. "I just helped you make sure you'd thought of crap that would occur to Martin. I know how his mind works."

"Yes, you do." She clapped. "How soon do you think we'll hear?"

"This afternoon," he assured. "There are only four other voting members, since I already cast my vote. Dave Danson is behind the project. I shot hoops with him yesterday."

"Wow, you really do plan ahead and think of everything."

"Good planning always has rewards." He shrugged. "Yours will come. I think you swayed Martin. After him, the other two should be a piece of cake. Honestly, I think they'll green-light you to start the focus groups quickly."

"That would be awesome. I still can't believe how well it went. If the project gets green-lighted, that will really help me refine the whole scope. With the feedback from the focus groups, I can capture what patrons in the identified demographics will want. If the data bears out my thoughts and these locations actually open, these will be more family-oriented than our current locations, but will—"

Noah grabbed her hands. "Sugar, you don't have to sell me. You persuaded me a long time ago."

"Thanks for believing I could." She bit her lip.

"I never doubted it."

Lauren smiled and looked up at him. His eyes sparkled with affection and sincerity. She sucked in a breath. Staring at that expression at such point-blank range was like being star-struck. It hit her square in the chest. God, he was so beautiful, it hurt.

Noah still held her hands in his. Warm. Slightly calloused. Large and longer-fingered. He was standing closer than ever. Dangerously close. And he was looking straight down at her. The room was suddenly thick with silence.

She swallowed.

The moment her stranger had slid deep in her body while she'd fantasized about Noah rushed back to her. Mr. Mysterious's touch made her blood hot, but when she'd conjured up a vision of Noah, he'd cranked up her blood to a roiling boil. The thought of him wanting her, binding her under him, and compelling her to accept his passion had sent her over the edge, head first into pleasure as sharp as a machete and so hot, lava felt like ice cubes by comparison.

Even remembering her fantasies made her blush.

"What are you thinking?" he asked, wearing a sexy smile that challenged her to tell the truth.

Oh, no. Did he have any idea that she was thinking about sex? With him?

Her bet? Yes. Time to lie like hell.

"A million things." She discreetly tugged her hands from his grasp and crossed the room to stuff the papers she'd brought from the meeting in her laptop case. "Gosh, doing well at this meeting was like a head rush, as amazing as an upside-down rollercoaster ride."

"The idea of beating up on Martin's intellect makes you blush? And here I thought maybe it was being close to me. I must be slipping."

Lauren heard his mocking tone, but still, she snapped her gaze up to his face. To his teasing smile that made her heart stop. Noah wasn't slipping. Since the day she'd become aware of him as a man a couple of years ago, she'd learned he was devastatingly effective against her resistance. If he ever turned the full force of his charm on her, she suspected he'd be lethal to her heart. Easily. After all, Noah had left a string of younger, sturdier hearts in his wake. She couldn't be stupid enough to add hers to his collection.

"You could never slip, Noah. But remember, I know you too well to fall for all that charm, so…" She shrugged and tried to toss him a light smile, then quickly segued to another subject by glancing at her watch. "Wow, look at the time. I didn't realize it was already almost eleven. I think I'll treat myself to an early lunch. Bye."

"Wait. I'll take you to lunch. You've more than earned it." He crossed the room to stand beside her again. "You can even have a glass of wine. I won't tell the boss," he whispered with a grin.

Lauren forced a laugh. What she really wanted to do was tear his clothes off. Bad, bad, bad idea.

"Let's go."

He placed a hand at the small of her back and guided her out the door. Lauren felt her nipples harden just from that inconsequential touch. She took a discreet half-step away from him.

"I need to collect my purse and stop at the restroom."

"I'll meet you in front of your desk in five."

Nodding, Lauren darted to the bathroom. Inside, she was blessedly alone and stared at herself in the mirror. The upswept do was professional. Her suit impeccable, thanks to her sister's great taste in clothing. The jewelry helped bring the look together for a casual sophistication that really was perfect for this office.

Unfortunately, her flushed cheeks, swollen lips and dilated eyes all screamed "fuck me".

Lauren groaned. She'd splash a sink full of cold water on her face if it wouldn't ruin her foundation and run her mascara.

Deep breaths, one after the other. She could do this. It was just lunch. Noah liked to tease, always had. His banter meant nothing. The fact she wanted his flirtation to…well, that was her problem.

Quickly, she used the facilities, washed her hands, returned to her desk and retrieved her purse. Noah stood quietly, waiting, watching. His gaze drilled her. Hot. Almost…like he wanted to strip her down and spend the afternoon between her legs. Surely he didn't mean to look at *her* that way. Impossible.

"Where to?" she asked brightly, hoping the sudden spike in her body temperature wasn't all over her face.

He suggested a nearby Mexican food restaurant, which she adored, and they were off. The car ride was tense. Lauren tried to fill it with conversation, but he kept sending *that* stare her way until she lost her train of thought and shut up.

They arrived at the restaurant and were seated right away. Again, Noah guided her across the place with a hand at the small of her back. His touch jolted her, vibrating through her, all the way down to her...better not to dwell on that part of her just now. Focusing on the wet ache would only kill her conversational skills.

Unfortunately, seated across from him, Lauren had almost nowhere to look except at Noah. She was never so grateful for a basket of tortilla chips so that she had something to do with her hands that didn't involve ripping that pristine white shirt from his yummy chest.

"You look tense, sugar. Relax and tell me what's wrong."

"Um, worried about the outcome of the meeting," she lied after swallowing her chip.

"It'll all come out in your favor. You watch."

Lauren suspected he was right, and she wasn't one to count her chickens. But she had to say something appropriate to the man. Somehow, she didn't think bringing up her midnight fantasies to him—about him—would be considered appropriate.

"Hey, while I've got you out and away from the office, can I ask you a question?"

She hesitated. "A question?"

"Yeah. Something personal."

Oh, this subject sounded ripe with possibilities, none of them good...

"Sure." What else could she say?

"I'm interested in this woman…"

"There's a shock."

Lauren winced as soon as she said it. Part pure sarcasm, part jealous annoyance, she hoped it hid her disappointment. This shouldn't upset her. At all. Noah and his sluts de jour were nothing new. It wasn't like she *loved* the man. Actually, she was more attached to him than was wise for her sanity, so maybe his pursuit of another woman was for the best.

Nice rationalization, she thought, restraining the urge to roll her eyes.

He laughed at her. Actually laughed! Unbelievable.

"I'm sure to you it looks like I've dated my fair share."

"Your share and half the male population in Texas's share. But whatever." She shrugged, pretending not to care.

The waiter came by and slapped glasses of water on their table, took their orders, and fled as only a busy man trying to keep up with the lunch rush could.

Once they were alone again, Noah continued, "This woman, she's divorced. And she's giving me the 'get lost' vibe. I'm not exactly sure why. Got any insider tips?"

"What, on the mind of a divorced woman?"

He nodded. "I mean, if you were her, why would you be blowing me off?"

"That's easy. Fear of pain. Divorce sucks. Relationships suck. They all end with someone hurting, and guys like you have no lasting power when it comes to matters of the heart, so she knows she's likely to be the one to be sitting at home with a bottle of wine, listening to sad country songs when it's all over. Given that fact, she's not going to take a chance on you, especially if you're still seeing Misty."

"Misty is out of the picture. She has been for a few weeks, actually."

Lauren was more pleased to hear that than she should be. "Still, your reputation proceeds you."

Noah hesitated, pretending to think. "But I don't think it's me she's objecting to. I think it's the idea of relationships in general. And I don't get it."

"Because clearly, you've never had your heart broken."

"I wouldn't say that."

To say Lauren was shocked was a huge understatement. "You, broken-hearted? I can't picture it."

"Try. I'm not impervious or immune. I've been hurt. Sometimes, it still hurts." He glanced away for a second, then shrugged. "That's never stopped me from dating and trying to move on. It's frustrating that she won't let her guard down with me. If you were her, what would be stopping you?"

"Aside from your cheerleaders and your reputation?"

Noah leaned forward, into her personal space, and directed her a stare that just about singed her toes. "Aside from that."

She tried to back away, but in a small restaurant booth, she really had no place to go. "I don't know this woman…"

"You're a lot like her, I think. You have a lot in common."

Lord, Lauren wanted to know who this woman was. And where did he meet her? A bar? A business trip? A bus stop? No telling.

"Look, I don't know her situation, so I probably shouldn't—"

"Please. I need your help. I really… This means a lot to me. She means a lot. I think she's the one."

Lauren sighed in defeat, grinding her teeth to try to hold in her…no, that couldn't be despair. She was upset. A little. That's it. Damn it.

Noah ditching his string of Miss Right-nows in favor of one Miss Right had to happen someday. The timing sucked, but she certainly didn't need a serious guy, much less another trip down the aisle. Maybe she should give him hints, send him on his way. Their office relationship would be much less strained if he had a serious someone else. Maybe she'd stop fantasizing about him. Someday.

She should help him…but the idea made her want to sharpen her fingernails and decorate this woman's face.

"Divorce taught me that men always want what's new and shiny," she whispered. "With Tim, it was promotions and trips to Rio and Moscow, Paris, Hong Kong, Cairo, etcetera. Fill in the blank. You get the picture. But the bottom line was, his work was always more important. He wasn't even there when Cass was born."

"I remember. I *was* there."

Her anger softened. "I know. It was sweet of you to wear out the carpet in the waiting room."

Amusement danced in his blue eyes. "Do you think she's afraid I might be a workaholic?"

"Not you. If she knows you at all, she knows that's not the problem. Focus, here. Shiny and new. With you, it's women. And with you, there's always plenty of those swarming around."

"I think swarming is a strong word."

"Yeah, you've never been crushed by the horde. Remember that Fourth of July picnic—"

"Ancient history," he insisted. "You're telling me you're convinced it's because she believes there'd be another woman to replace her sooner or later."

"Sooner *rather* than later. Even if she isn't specifically worried about you leaving her for someone else, it takes a while before a girl wants to risk her heart again. God knows, I'm in no hurry."

Noah shot her a piercing stare. "But what if, in your hesitance, you're passing up Mr. Perfect-for-you?"

Lauren paused. That had never actually occurred to her. Clearly, she was too young to spend the rest of her life alone. She might be ready for a steady boyfriend in the next decade. But what about all the opportunities—men—she was passing up now?

"I guess if it was meant to be, he could wait until I was ready."

Noah shook his head. "What if he's ready now? Take me, for instance. I'm almost forty. I want a wife and babies while I'm young enough to enjoy them."

Her jaw dropped so low, Lauren felt sure it dragged on the table. "You want to marry this woman and have kids?"

"Yes." He stared at her. Right at her.

That stare unnerved her. She swallowed. Here came that nasty imitation of despair again. But boy, it felt like the real thing… "I had no idea you were that serious."

"Now you do."

"What about the woman who once broke your heart?"

"Who says this isn't the same woman?"

Okie dokie. He was serious. Deadly serious. Lauren blew out a deep breath. She could handle the fact Noah had apparently been in love with someone for at least months, maybe years, without crying. Hopefully.

"And you're just going to take another chance on this same woman, even though she hurt you the first time?"

"Lying to myself about what's in my heart isn't going to make me happy."

Lauren had to give Noah credit. That made sense. "Have you told her how you feel?"

He shook his head. "If some guy told you he wanted to waltz you down the aisle and was hoping for a quick trip to the maternity ward, would you run screaming in the other direction?"

"Totally."

"There you go."

Lauren sighed. Damn, he was smart. A master strategist in all areas of life and damn good at it. She wondered if the woman would even notice that he'd planned her life for her until it was too late. Noah was also good-looking, fun, rich, and she'd heard, great in bed. He'd catch this woman eventually. While Lauren knew she'd still be alone.

She pushed that thought aside.

"*If* you remarried, hypothetically, would you have more babies?" he asked into her maudlin silence.

Good question, even though the thought of Noah having babies with his unnamed divorcée bitch made her want to crawl into a gallon of Häagen-Dazs and never come out. "Probably. I love kids, and if this hypothetical marriage took place soon, my little ones are still fairly young, so all the kids would likely play together. Does this woman already have kids?"

Noah never answered. The food arrived, and he set into his with a fork and a vengeance.

"Good stuff," he said after the first mouthful.

Lauren took a bite and wished she could agree. But in her mind, she could only see some nameless, faceless centerfold-type hanging on Noah, wearing a huge diamond on her left hand, with two perfect kids trailing behind, not a hair out of place.

Utterly depressing. She really had to snap out of it and be happy that Noah had finally found someone he wanted to spend his life with. It was probably better that Lauren had no idea who this paragon of femininity was. She could hate the woman without feeling an ounce of guilt.

They finished the meal in relative silence. After Noah paid the bill and refused to let her buy her own lunch, they stood. He anchored his hand in the small of her back again as they crossed the restaurant, to the parking lot.

"Thanks for the talk at lunch. You really helped me to understand."

She nodded and tried to smile. Confessing her misery over the fact Noah was plotting to marry another woman was not an option. "Glad to help."

Wow, it was a miracle she didn't choke over that lie.

"You confirmed all my suspicions."

"Suspicions?"

"Clearly, I need to convince this woman that I'm for real." He glanced down at her with a mischievous smile. "And I've already got ideas."

Lauren wished his centerfold divorcée luck. Personally, she didn't think the woman had a prayer in hell of resisting.

ଔ ଔ ଔ

Back at the office, Lauren and Noah arrived just in time to see a delivery man set a huge bouquet of multi-colored roses on her desk. Red, white, pink, yellow. What the…?

Noah stood propped against the wall, arms crossed over that wide chest of his, watching with a quirked brow. "Wow, you must have rocked Mr. Mysterious's world."

She shook her head. "There has to be some mistake."

Surely Mr. Mysterious hadn't sent these. *Why not?* a voice in her head asked. He'd delivered his other notes here.

"I don't think there's any mistake, sugar. Read the card."

With trembling fingers, Lauren plucked the little sealed envelope from its plastic fork. Damn, having the man she lusted after—and whose heart was apparently now taken—watch as she read a message from the man who'd screwed her into the mattress and rocked *her* world was uncomfortable. Bordering on the insane.

Lauren extracted the card and read, her eyes widening with every word.

I loved making love to you. There's a bloom here for every time I'm going to do it again this week…

She blinked, stared at the bouquet, and took a quick count. She stopped at eight, realizing she was just over half through. The man thought he was going to make love to her a dozen times this week?

No. Oh, no. A dozen times with that man, fueled by fantasies of Noah, and her body would be sore, her mind mush, and her heart… She shook her head, refusing to think about it.

"What does it say?" Noah asked, sauntering over and reaching out to snatch the card from her.

"You're nosy. Give that back!"

He ignored her. As he read the card, she closed her eyes and vowed to buy an industrial paper shredder and drag it into her cubicle so he wouldn't read anything else her stranger wrote for her eyes alone.

Noah's gaze lifted from the card, then drifted over the bouquet. "Ambitious guy. Think he can...follow through?"

Wishing a vast hole would open and swallow her whole, but knowing it wasn't going to happen, she closed her eyes, swallowed, and nodded. "Yeah."

"Hmm. You went from red to green, back to red again. Hot and bothered, I get. But sick?"

"I'm not green. I'm fine."

"Yeah? And I'm the Easter Bunny. Why does the idea of being with Mr. Mysterious make you sick?"

"You may be in the mood to discuss your love life. I, however, am not. Can we drop it?"

"Sugar, if you don't want this guy, the next time you see him, there's one word that will take care of him. It's no. Just say no."

Lauren felt the red recede in favor of the green again when her stomach flipped. How could she explain this? "It's not that simple. I— He..." She blew out a breath. "He's very...skilled."

He chuckled. "Newsflash, Lauren. Sex is meant to feel good. If he's skilled and it's hot between you two, be happy. But if he's hurting you—"

"No. He's not hurting me."

"What's the problem?"

"You'll laugh."

"I won't. Promise. Lay it on me."

She shook her head. "That's okay. Maybe we should check in with your assistant to see if the rest of the owners' committee has come to a decision."

When Lauren started to walk away, Noah grabbed her elbow and pulled her back to him. Very close to him. So close she could see the various colors of blue and gray swirling in his eyes as he stared down at her. Feel the heat of his body. She stared at his firm mouth like a half-drooling idiot and wondered what it would be like to kiss him.

"You helped me at lunch," he reminded her. "Let me help you."

He looked so sincere, Lauren didn't know how to say no. Maybe he *could* help her. Heaven knew he had more than enough experience in the bedroom department, if rumors were true.

Lauren sighed. Why not go for broke? "Being with him…it messes with my head," she whispered. "He forces me to feel things I—I've never felt. We connected."

"That's not a bad thing," he assured softly.

"I'm not ready."

"You and Tim split up almost two years ago. You've got to jump into the dating game sometime."

"With a man who won't tell me his name? I've never seen his face even. Gary offered to take me to dinner and a movie. That's more my speed."

Noah's expression hardened. "No, it's not. That gives you too much opportunity to put up barriers. Mr. Mysterious is getting to you. It's uncomfortable, but if you do it Gary's way, you'd be old enough to collect Social Security before you ever let a man back in your heart."

As much as it made her want to scream, Noah was right. "I don't want another man in my heart."

"Lauren—"

Noah's leggy, thirty-something assistant, Jennifer, approached them. Lauren would have been annoyed at his choice of secretaries if it wasn't a well-known fact that Jenn had been very happily married for almost fifteen years.

"Mr. Reeves, Ms. Southall, the committee is on the phone. They're asking to speak to you. Oh, and I dropped off your cleaning at your house."

Lauren's stomach did a flip-flop as Noah nodded. Uh-oh. The moment of truth. This project meant so much to her—the first big one Noah had assigned to her since she'd joined the company. She wanted to prove to her detractors that it wasn't just nepotism. And prove to Noah that he hadn't made a mistake.

"Thanks. Hang onto the key, just in case." At Jenn's murmured assent, Noah went on, "We'll take the call in my office. Hold all calls and visitors for now."

Lauren's belly did another flip. She'd be well and truly alone with a man who, with a single thought of him, could get her hot. Now she wasn't sure if she was more anxious about that or the committee's decision.

Noah touched a hand to the small of her back to guide her to his office. That innocent little touch set off all kinds of receptors in her body. Geez, she survived without sex for two years, but the minute she got some…she only wanted more. Pitiful.

Side-stepping Noah, she made her way to his office. Her heart suddenly double-timed as he shut the door behind them.

"Ready?" His eyes danced with mischief.

Staring at his expression, it wasn't hard to imagine he was asking if she was ready for something X-rated. If he'd asked that question, the answer was hell yes. Totally pitiful.

"Sure. Let's hear the decision." She sank into the chair in front of his desk.

Walking behind the desk, Noah eased into his own chair and pressed the button on his speakerphone. "Reeves here. I've got Lauren with me. Go."

"Glad you're both available," Danson said. "Lauren, you did a great job today."

"Thank you, sir."

"You brought up points that Noah didn't mention Sunday afternoon when he took me aside to persuade me after wiping the basketball court with my ass."

"I didn't wipe the court with your ass," Noah argued. "I pressed my height advantage."

Noah was easily six-foot-three. Danson might be five-eight on a good day.

"Yeah, and you used it to wipe the court with my ass. Anyway..." he huffed good-naturedly, "...we're green-lighting the project research. Four focus groups each in the three demographics we discussed. They're welcome to come to any of the locations and order anything on the menu, as long as they come at the appointed time and answer questions directly afterward. I know you wanted them to come during the weekends and dinner hours, but we can't let this disrupt our usual business."

Lauren clenched her fists and pumped one in the air. Victory! The dining time was a small set-back, but easily worked around.

"Thank you. To all of the committee."

"You know I was your toughest critic," Martin chimed in. "But the income projections you provided, coupled with the low-cost location modifications to support a family environment you researched, convinced me to give it a try."

Exactly as Noah said. She was so excited, she was nearly bouncing in her seat.

"Yes, sir. I think you'll see the restaurant-goers in that area will love the idea of casual elegance in dining that does its best to include the kids. I suspect the extensive wine list will be a big hit, as well as the additions of Sunday brunches."

"Get us hard data and we'll look at it again."

"I'll get started right away. I have the plan for the focus groups in place. We can have everything completed in the next few weeks."

"Great, Lauren." Danson again. "Congratulations."

"Thanks to all of you. I won't disappoint."

After a quick round of good-byes, Noah clicked the speakerphone button and stood. Silence spread over the room as he stood and looked at her with an indulgent smile. She couldn't stand the excitement another minute. She bounced out of her chair and darted for him. Thrilled as hell, she grabbed his shoulders and raised on her tip-toes to place a kiss on his cheek.

At the last second, he turned his head and her lips pressed right against his.

Lauren froze. Her heart stopped. She didn't pull away. She should, but... His lips were soft yet firm as he paused over her mouth, warm but unmoving. Unable to resist, she leaned in. A heartbeat passed, then another. Heat swamped her. He didn't pull away, and she moved her lips over his, brushing, then fusing them together, dying for a taste of him.

An electric jolt charged her, slamming her brain, her breath. Lauren jumped away. Shock hummed, sudden arousal buzzed.

What the hell had she done? Her mouth hung open, and she was dimly aware of gaping.

"I'm so sorry. I didn't mean to... I was just excited."

A naughty smile lifted the corner of wide mouth. "I've never had a woman apologize to me before for being excited. Please don't be the first."

"I meant about the project results." A raging blush swept up her chest, neck, all the way to the roots of her hair. She felt the heat climbing up, and again, cursed her fair-skinned features.

"Okay."

Lauren couldn't tell whether he thought she was lying or just poking fun at her mortification to lighten the moment. She pressed her hand to her chest and stared at him in horror. "You're my boss, and that was so unprofessional."

"We're friends, too. I hardly minded. It was a peck."

Noah was playing this cool. Why couldn't she?

"True. Just a peck." With enough power to light up Times Square—and everything else in a ten block radius. "It won't happen again."

"Oh, don't restrain yourself on my account." He smiled and winked.

Did he really mean that? He couldn't. But if he did...what about the woman he wanted to marry?

"You're a big flirt." Truer words were never spoken. And his teasing didn't mean anything...no matter how much she wanted it to.

"We all have to excel at something." He grinned. "Speaking of which, Tim told me that Cass is still learning how to swim and needs practice. I think my pool is finally warm enough, and it doesn't get nearly enough use. Do you want to bring the girls over tonight? We can swim and order pizza or barbeque. Your choice."

Damn. Double-damn! Cass loved the pool and did need the practice. But after that awkward kiss, the last thing she needed to do was go to his house and spend the evening staring at Noah's prime, smoking-hot bod in a bathing suit.

Lauren was heartily glad to be able to truthfully say, "Thanks for the invitation. It's sweet of you to let my two rascals splash around in your pool. But we can't."

"Big plans with Mr. Mysterious?"

She glared. "No. My mom picked up the girls from school and they're going to spend a few days there. She and Walter just got back from her Caribbean cruise and she said she missed them to pieces. I missed her, too, and told her I'd have dinner over there."

"Maybe another night this week? You name the day."

The follow-up invitation surprised her. But if the kiss hadn't ruffled his view of their friendship, she supposed that it shouldn't change hers, either. It couldn't. They'd been friends for too long to let this sudden, weird lust usurp her usual fondness for him.

"Thursday? I'll be done with my yoga class by 6:30 if that's not too late."

"Perfect. It's a date."

Date? As in man-woman seeing each other to find out if they're compatible conversationally…and otherwise?

No. Certainly he didn't mean it was a date-date. Just that they'd set the date for them to get together. Who took their children on a first date-date? No one. She relaxed.

"Um...yes. See you then."

"Have fun with Mr. Mysterious tonight."

Lauren rolled her eyes. "I told you, I have no plans to see the man tonight."

"Given how many roses there were in that bouquet and the note he sent you, I have a hunch he plans to see you. Lots of you." He grinned. "I hope you're ready."

Chapter Six

Night fell over the April evening when Noah let himself into Lauren's house. Quiet. Dark. Empty. Exactly as he'd thought; she'd left work and gone straight to see her mother, Walter, and the girls. She'd have dinner there, maybe stay long enough to help bathe and tuck Emma and Cass into bed.

When she got home, Mr. Mysterious would be waiting for her.

Noah glanced at his watch. Almost nine o'clock. She'd be here soon. He needed to be ready to steal into her body and keep working his way into her heart the moment she walked in the door—before she had more time to build back her defenses.

After today, moving quickly and playing smart were imperative, since he'd made some very interesting observations. First, she was jumpy around him. And the way she'd impulsively kissed him—and lingered over it—before jumping away guiltily...very telling. Her expression when he'd announced his interest in and intent to marry another divorcée had given him broad hints about her feelings, too. Lauren tried to look unaffected, but seeing her face to face, she was as capable of hiding her emotions as she was at suppressing a blush. In other words, not at all.

Putting all those clues together, he'd bet every dollar he had that she was aware of him, not just as a boss or as a pal, but as a man. A definite cause for a rousing halleluiah.

In the not-so-good-news category, though, was having to lie to her about having another woman in his heart. If she feared he'd leave her for some other female, he hated to add to her reasons to avoid him. But perversely, the lie would help her assume she was "safe" from him. She'd let her guard down and continue giving him hints that would help him conquer her. He'd absolve her of the ridiculous notion that he had no sexual or romantic interest in her when the time was right.

But there was more bad news: her adamant declaration she that wasn't going to fall in love again. She was lying to herself, protecting herself, and Noah knew it. But convincing her would be one of his biggest challenges in this scheme.

At least Noah understood now exactly why she was resisting him. Every girl he'd ever dated and bedded in his vain attempt to forget Lauren was coming back to haunt him. Damn it to hell. He couldn't change the past, so he had to work with the hand he'd dealt himself. She'd learn that he wouldn't chase after someone shinier. To him, she was as bright as a thousand suns, and he would do whatever necessary to convince her of his sincerity and love.

With help from Mr. Mysterious.

After hearing her confession that being with her midnight stranger made her feel uncommonly connected to him, Noah had hid his smile—and his killer erection—barely.

But tonight, very soon, he'd feel free to grin like an idiot and introduce her to the iron hard-on plaguing him even now. He'd connect with her in every way he could. Then, when the time was right, he'd tell her that Noah and Mr. Mysterious were one and the same. By then, she'd know they were compatible on every level, and helping her accept the relationship would be a snap.

Locking the door behind him, Noah pulled out a flashlight from the black bag he brought with him and looked around the house. She usually came in through the garage and laundry room into the rest of the house. From there, she could either wind her way to her bedroom via a path to the right of the stairs and through the kitchen, or left of the stairs, through the dining room. Sure, he could wait until she entered the bedroom, but his goal here was to continually surprise her, keep her off balance, always guessing…and panting.

Striding to the laundry room door, he stared at his options, glancing both ways around the stairs in front of him. Dining room, he decided, striding through the formal area and to the front door, where he flipped on the porch lights. Lauren would come this way to investigate once she drove up and saw those lights on.

Decision made, Noah strode back into the shadowed living room and switched off the flashlight. Darkness closed around him, but he didn't need much light to work. He set his bag beside the silk ficus tree in the corner, placed a few necessary goodies in one of the chairs lining the side of the rectangular table, then pulled the head chair two feet away from the table, toward the ficus tree. Then he worked his way into the corner, behind the silk tree. And waited.

෨ ෨ ෨

Lauren dropped her keys on the counter in the laundry room and dragged herself a few steps forward. She felt her way out of the room, too tired to care about the dark and too familiar with the house to bother with lights.

A faint cast of moonlight made its way through the kitchen windows, illuminating her stairs. She turned left, frowning. She'd noticed the porch lights on when she'd driven up. Had she left them on last night? Maybe her mother had stopped by here earlier and turned them on.

As if your electric bill isn't high enough…

As she walked through the dining room, feeling her way through the dark, she reached a hand out to steady herself on the chair at the head of the table.

It wasn't in its place, but she could make out the outline of it a couple of feet away.

First the porch light was on, and now a chair out of place? Unusual. Hardly anyone ever used this room. Were all the weird occurrences her unofficial welcome to the Twilight Zone?

Awareness prickled along her spine suddenly. Lauren swore she could hear someone exhale. Raggedly. Goosebumps raised on her arms, getting bigger as her heart raced faster.

Or was it possible she wasn't alone? Maybe Mr. Mysterious was here, waiting to make good on his plan to ravish her body once for each bloom in that awesome bouquet she'd received earlier today.

Lauren reached for the chair. "Hello?"

Nothing. But suddenly, she *felt* him here. Yes, she was tired, and it was possible her imagination was overactive…but she didn't think so.

Her heart raced like it was finishing the final laps at the Indy 500. Bracing herself on the chair, she made to walk out of the dining room and into the foyer to flip on a light. She'd told him to leave Friday night. The man coming back…not a good idea. He would only take her body and mess with her head, if she let him.

She wasn't about to allow that.

A firm hand clamped around her wrist before she got anywhere near the light switch and pulled, jerking her back against the hot width of his male chest.

Electricity shot down her arm, exploded in her body. She gasped in the darkness. Oh, God. He *was* back. Here. And given the erect cock prodding her backside, Lauren didn't have to guess twice what he had in mind.

"Hello, Lauren," he whispered in her ear. "I told you I'd be back."

Mr. Mysterious. And she knew what he wanted. His sin-infused voice rasped against her senses. Like the devil's, his voice seemed to say that he'd returned not just to possess her body but to steal her soul. Adrenaline pumped into her and morphed into arousal that snaked through her mercilessly.

His other hand journeyed from her waist up, up—until his palm smoothed over her breast.

"Hard nipples. Nice welcome. For me?"

His touch was like fire. She swallowed against the zip of pleasure slinking up her spine. "Who are you?"

He tsked at her. "We've already played that game. Now's not the time to rehash it again. I'm here to play something far more interesting."

"But I never got an answer."

"All in good time." As if he knew his answer would piss her off, he tempered the words with a seductive caress of his lips over the sensitive crook of her neck. His fingertips skated over her nipples. Her knees buckled.

"You shouldn't be here." Her voice shook.

"You're right. I shouldn't be here." He nudged his hard cock against the small of her back. "I should be…"

The hand he'd anchored at her waist dipped south. Lauren's belly fluttered as his palm glided over her flesh. Heat blossomed inside her as his fingers inched slowly toward the damp, aching spot between her legs.

He covered her mound with his enormous hand. "Here. Right here."

"No," she choked past her urge to whimper and beg.

What was it about the man's touch? Like an electric kaleidoscope of color and sensation. One touch and she could barely remember her own name, much less resist.

"Did you like your roses?" His hushed voice teased, taunted, made her shiver.

"Yes." She heard the tremble in her voice. "But what you want…it's not possible."

His wicked chuckle in her ear sent a shiver through her. He palmed the flat of her belly, bringing her even closer to him. "It's inevitable."

Warm, moist lips trailed a path of kisses from her ear down to her shoulder. His hot breath heated her, stirring across her skin. Lauren shivered.

"I love the feel of you trembling for me. I want to feel that tonight as I fuck you." He nipped on her lobe. "As I make love to you."

"No," she protested.

But it was weak. Very weak. Already, his body heat and her memories were combining to crush her resistance. His mouth at her neck drumming up her desires helped to make her self-control look like a tin can freshly crushed for recycling.

"Yes. You're special. I want to show you that, give you the kind of pleasure you've never had."

"You already have. Friday night was amazing, but—"

"Friday night was just a start. I'm dying to give you more. Everything."

Lauren exhaled raggedly. Everything? She didn't doubt he could. If he did, however, she feared her heart and her body wouldn't be hers anymore by the time he was done.

"I already said no."

"I respect that word," he promised. "But not when you're quivering in my arms and creaming your panties while you say it."

Damn! He knew she wanted him.

Of course he knew. The man wasn't an idiot. He was a single-minded, sexually-driven god between the sheets, his hard body was well equipped to drive a woman to repeated orgasms.

And you're resisting…why? Her sex drive asked.

Her sex drive was not helping her keep her priorities straight.

"That isn't the point. I'm not ruled by my panties."

"Ruled? No. But let's see if your panties and I can *persuade* you…"

Before Lauren could breathe or form a coherent answer, Mr. Mysterious had reached beneath her suit skirt and grabbed the panties in question. With a good yank, he ripped them away and tossed them to the ground.

"You don't wear those again this week, day or night. I want to know that pretty pussy is bare and waiting for me all day."

"At work—"

"No one at work will know." He froze. "Unless you plan on showing someone you work with."

Lauren's mind flooded with images of Noah—smiling, frowning in thought, shooting her a heated stare. Instead of ramping her desire down, the thought of giving Noah a glimpse of her bare, wet sex made her desire spike fiercely.

"Do you?" he demanded.

"N—no," she stammered. "But that doesn't mean I'm going to show you."

"Oh?" He slipped his fingers into her wet slit, right over her clit and gave a soft little slide. "You're this wet and needy but you plan to ease yourself?"

As if she could… Only he made her ache like this. Damn him.

Even now, those fingers of his, just grazing her clit slowly, rhythmically, slowly destroyed her defiance—and sanity. The coil of need wrapped tighter and tighter low in her belly, right between her legs. She bit her lip to keep from crying out.

But he knew.

"Don't hold it in. I want you to tell me how you feel."

"Stop," she grated out.

He did. Instantly. His fingers ceased their lush, leisurely stimulation. But his fingers remained on her hard clit, which pulsed under his touch, silently begging. The ache between her legs became a clamp of pleasure/pain at the sudden deprivation of his strokes.

Nothing in the world could stop the whimper that clawed up her throat and out of her mouth.

"I know," he murmured gruffly. "I feel you throbbing under my fingers. It's the same way my cock throbs for you. Want me to make it better, sugar?"

Sugar. Noah called her that. Always had. Mr. Mysterious wasn't Noah, who was apparently off chasing some divorcée who was too stubborn to see what a prize the man was. But with Mr. Mysterious's build and deep whisper, there was enough similarity between the two men. She could pretend Noah had his hands on her now, tempting her into the white-hot pleasure that was just a whisper of his fingertips away.

Lauren wrestled with herself. Her body versus her mind. The preservation of her heart against the wailing demands of her clit.

It wasn't a contest.

"Yes."

His fingers twitched—just enough to send the ache between her legs skyrocketing for an instant. "You sure?"

"Damn you, do it!"

A slick glide of fingers, a gentle pinch of her clit. She gasped, air burning her throat at the quick intake. Her head fell back against his hard shoulder. She melted into him.

"Do what?" Now his thumb entered the action, brushing right over the exposed bead of her clit. A line of pure fire shot from her sex down her legs, up her spine, to her breasts. Lord, what this man could do to her...

"Make me come. Fuck me."

"I'm going to make you come. But I won't fuck you until you're so wet, your thighs are dripping with cream. And then...I'll make love to you."

Alarm bells went off in some distant part of Lauren's brain, but she was lost in the blazing sensations, the way they seared her everywhere. Lost in the fantasy of Noah being the man behind her, fondling her into delirium.

He kicked her thighs farther apart, hooking his feet inside her ankles to keep them wide until he was nearly supporting her entire body. The hand toying with her clit slid down to her slick opening. He plunged a pair of fingers inside her. Immediately, she clamped down on him to trap his fingers inside, her whole channel aware of him and craving his next touch. Lauren arched, bucking into his invasion. His fingers sank deeper, and she groaned. Close. So damn close...

"Not yet," he taunted. "Unbutton your blouse for me first."

Despite her trembling fingers, Lauren tore into those buttons so quickly, she was sure she set some sort of record. Within a few seconds, the blouse hung open all the way to her waist.

"That bra better unclasp in the front."

She could hear him panting now. His whisper was strained, and Lauren felt a measure of victory to know she was affecting him. Even as a niggle of worry needled her.

"It doesn't."

He swore. "Bend over. Brace your elbows on the table."

Oh, God. He was going to spread her across her own table and fuck her from behind. Tim had never done that. Tim had never taken her outside the bedroom.

With his body, he urged her down. Lauren had no choice but to do as he said or fall on her face.

Oh, who was she kidding, the thought of being taken this way made her sex cramp in hunger, her belly jump in anticipation. Breathing? More difficult with every passing moment.

At the soft thud of her elbows making contact with the table, he used his free hand to strip off her shirt and bra, jerking them down her arms and to the floor, in about two seconds flat. As soon as he was done, he settled his palm over her breast, gripping her nipple with ruthless fingers. The other hand started working her slick channel again, thumb brushing over her clit in short, mind-melting caresses.

As she gasped, Lauren realized she now wore nothing but her skirt. He was still fully dressed. He'd made her his to conquer, his to use, his to bend to his will.

Noah would be this way with a woman, dominant, skillful, in control. He'd do exactly what Mr. Mysterious was doing now, working her sensitive sheath with fingers that knew exactly where to press to make her lose her breath, lose her mind. Imagining it was Noah only made her ache more.

Building and building, the sensations threatened to consume her. Shivers of excitement danced down her spine and settled between her legs, winding tight. Becoming a peak of sensitivity. Blood flowed, filling her up. Almost...

"You going to come for me?" he growled.

"Yes," she breathed, high and tight, almost keening the word.

He pinched her nipple, thumbed her clit, pressed against that magic spot deep inside her. "Let go. I want to feel you on my fingers."

Lauren couldn't have stopped the tidal wave of sensation for any reason. His hands, those words—and her restraint evaporated. A high-pitched wail echoed through the house, across the hardwood floors. Her throat hurt even as pleasure was clawing at the rest of her body in a searing press of need that never relented. That was her screaming, her needing, her coming...and coming.

Behind her, Mr. Mysterious groaned and ground his cock into the crack of her ass. "You're so fucking sexy. I jacked off many times thinking about how you'd sound when you came."

His words filled her with a forbidden thrill. She'd made a lover of his caliber so needy he'd taken his own flesh in his hand. She had to see it. See him.

"Show me."

He stilled for a long moment. "Soon. Right now, taste."

After a long drag of his fingers through her humid center that made her groan again, he withdrew his fingers and raised them to her mouth.

"No."

"Taste," he demanded.

Lauren shook her head.

"I want you to taste, so you can't deny my effect on you."

The urgency of his whispered demand aroused her again. His dominant side reached something deep inside her. She wanted to please him. She wanted more of the stunning, shimmering erotic bombshell he delivered. Anything, everything he could give her. He'd never have to know that she responded so easily because she imagined Noah jacking off while desperately wondering what she sounded like when she cried out from the pleasure he gave her.

Slowly, she parted her lips. He glossed her bottom lip with her thick fluids and he reached into a bag at his feet. He rummaged around, pulled a scrap of cloth out with his free hand.

"Turn to face me," he demanded.

Lauren whirled, hoping to see his face. And yet, hoping not to. If she didn't know who this man was, she could preserve the fantasy that Noah was here demanding every wicked act she'd pondered deep in her psyche during the restless nights she wore out the batteries on her vibrator.

He stood there. Tall. Definitely over six feet by a few inches. Broad. No stranger to hard work or the gym or both. Shoulders so wide they eclipsed the doorway to the foyer and any light that might shine through.

But no face.

He wore a ski mask, with cutouts for his eyes, nose, and mouth. She knew nothing more about him than she'd known before except that he had a wide mouth that made her ache for kisses and he didn't have dark eyes. They were pale and glittered with hunger that took her breath away.

"Lick it off your lip," he demanded. "Taste yourself."

Shyly, her tongue peeked out to swipe across her lip. Salty-sweet. Musky. A surprise.

A smile lifted one corner of his mouth. "Beautiful. Open up."

He raised the two fingers that had been deep in her sex to her mouth. She swallowed, her wide, uncertain gaze snagging on his. The firm encouragement there, the knowledge that the sight of his wet fingers on her tongue would drive him wild lay in those depths.

Lauren parted her lips, sucked his fingers inside. More of her taste bombarded her senses. She should probably be repulsed, but it was hard to feel anything but a thrill when his eyes narrowed and he hissed in a breath as if he teetered on the edge of restraint.

The idea of shoving him over the edge made her pulse with forbidden thrill.

She swirled her tongue around his fingers until she tasted nothing but his skin. Her gaze was locked on him, and she couldn't look away as desire whipped through his eyes, tightened his lips, made his body taut.

"You're a minx." His gravel voice rasped across her senses. "And I would love to feel that sweet tongue on my cock, but I'm not going to be able to keep out of your pussy long enough tonight."

Mr. Mysterious grabbed her, moved her toward the table. Lauren resisted. The idea of tasting him raced through her blood with potent wine.

"Wait. You promised I could see you touch yourself." She'd never been forward or vocal, and she felt wildly brazen now.

"Definitely a minx." He shot her a sizzling grin as he reached for the snap of his black jeans.

It gave way under his deft fingers. His zipper descended in a slow rasp that cut through the thick air and sent shivers racing over her skin. Lauren gritted her teeth, wanting to tell him to move faster. He would only deny her. Instead, she tensed, balling her fists as impatience screamed under her skin.

Finally, he finished and pushed his jeans around his hips. His cock sprang into his hands.

Lauren wished she could see more than an outline of him. In shadow, he looked long and thick. She could just make out the shape of his hand slowly pumping, his thumb dragging along his length and nudging the crown.

But that wasn't enough. She wanted more, to touch him, take him into her hands, her mouth…

Reaching for him, Lauren grasped his silken heat. She gripped him tight—and still couldn't get her fingers all the way around him. Oh, God!

He groaned deep in his chest as he dropped his hand to his side. Lauren stroked the rigid shaft, her fingers finding roped veins running up and down the impressive, velvet-steel length.

It was like holding thunder. She could feel the power pulsing in her hand every time she dragged her fingers up his cock, then plunged them back down. Friction and heat seared her palm. He moaned again and, with a yank on her arm, pulled her closer, his mouth capturing hers, tongue thrusting inside and ravaging her. She shivered and moaned as she met the fire in his kiss, but she didn't just melt. She met him with a blaze of her own and overshadowed his ruthless demands by massaging his cock in long strokes. With her other hand, she cupped his testicles.

They were heavy and drawing taut as she fondled them. She relished holding him, his power, in her palm. He relished it, too, pumping his erection into her tight fist and tearing his mouth from hers in an effort to breathe.

"God, I've dreamed of this. Of your hands on me."

"You feel amazing," she said on another smooth upstroke that made him gasp.

"I'd rather feel amazing inside you, but if you keep that up, I'm going to come."

Her stranger grabbed her wrists and snatched her hands from his cock.

"But—"

Her protest found no more voice than that before he propped her ass up on the table and pressed her backwards, laying her out across the gleaming surface. The wood was cold against her heated skin. She hissed, but he pushed a hand to the center of her chest to keep her down.

"Hot and cold," he murmured on her ear. "Soft…" He skimmed his fingertips across her breasts, against her tight, aching nipples. "And hard."

His mask-covered head traveled down, down, until his lips poised about her breast. He sucked the hard tip inside the stunning heat of his mouth, then bit down. Not hard—but enough to make her sizzle and scream. She felt the jolt all the way to her vagina.

He repeated the action with her other breast, sucking and biting one, alternately pinching and soothing the other. Back and forth, over and over, he paid attention to her breasts until she felt them swell, felt her sex ache again. Lauren had never felt such violent sensations in her breasts. Never swelled so much she could swear she felt his every exhalation tighten her nipples even more. Panting, on fire, she arched up. A plea sat on the tip of her tongue.

Lauren reached up to grab his head and keep him in place. The yarn under her hands frustrated her. She wanted to feel his hair. Dark hair. Noah's hair.

Immediately, he grabbed her wrists and shoved them back to the table. "The mask stays."

Desire and confusion all whirled through her at once. She nodded. "I just wanted to touch you."

The tension in his body released. "Soon. I want that, too. But tonight, I want deep inside you. I want to be in so tight you can't feel anything but my cock."

"Yes," she moaned. "I want you inside me." *Noah…*

The words barely left her lips before he lifted her against the hard width of chest, set her on her feet, then spun her around. She faced the table, feelings churning through her so quickly she could barely process them. Desire. Oh, yes. Tightly strung, achy, need scraped at her patience. She felt raw, ready to scream. She had no idea how a man she didn't know could affect her so easily and deeply, and she was beyond caring.

Fear. Lord, she almost didn't recognize herself. She wasn't the kind of woman to have sex with a stranger. On her own dining room table. She wasn't the kind of woman to beg. But the desire overpowered the fear. Handily.

And she whispered, "Fuck me."

He slid his cock against her, but instead of entering her, he dragged his length along her slick folds, then began bumping her clit in a soft rhythm, rubbing her with the head in a smooth motion designed to devastate until she wanted to scream.

"Are you wet enough?"

Wet enough? Was he out of his mind? Her sex felt incredibly swollen and her inner thighs were wet with her own juices. With every breath and every movement, she could feel her bare flesh rubbing against itself. It was driving her crazy. And with his cock rooting around her aching sex, he was driving her crazy.

"You know I am."

"How bad do you want it?" he whispered against her neck.

Fresh shivers wracked her. Frustration boiled up. She wiggled her ass at him, trying to entice, trying to trip the head of his cock inside her. He evaded, kept teasing and stroking her clit with his erection.

"I want it," she panted.

"Enough to beg?"

Beg? Oh, that sounded terrible…and wonderful. She'd never wanted anything bad enough to beg for it, but he was pushing her every button, shoving her closer and closer to insanity. This dominant man and his forceful behavior reminded her of Noah. He made her feel like a wild woman prowled inside her, dying to burst free.

"Do you?" he prodded, pinching her nipples with his hands.

Easy capitulation had never been her style, however. And some feminine instinct told her he'd enjoy the hell out of her defiance. "Just fuck me."

He chuckled in her ear. "Big girl thinks she's calling all the shots now? I've got news for you. You're bent over a table with your ass in

Shelley Bradley

the air. I could spank your pretty cheeks pink, and you couldn't stop me."

Mr. Mysterious reached a hand between them, then plunged a finger into her tight depths. Instantly, her body clasped at his finger, trying to suck him deeper. When he pressed down on her G-spot, she moaned and arched into his hand.

But he didn't stay, damn him. Instead, he withdrew and trailed his finger from her swollen opening back to her anus. She stiffened when he circled her tight, unbreached hole with his wet digit.

"I could fuck you here."

But he didn't. He just continued rimming the small hole with his finger, awakening nerve endings she'd never known existed, then he plunged inside.

A gasp tore from her throat. Sensations she'd never dreamed of swarmed her. Her knees went weak, and Lauren was damn glad to have a table under her to hold her weight.

His finger filled her up, and he rhythmically pumped her ass with it. Friction bit into her resistance and heat shimmied up her spine. Every thrust of his finger seemed to send a fresh ache straight to her pussy, right to her clit. She pressed back against his hand, seeking more of the delicious stimulation threatening her sanity.

"Oh my God." Her voice trembled.

"No one has ever touched you here."

It wasn't a question. It was as if he knew the answer. "No. Never."

"I'm going to do more than touch you. I'll fuck you here. Soon."

The idea seared her with a bolt of heat. The ache in her belly tightened. She'd never fantasized about being anally penetrated. But after her stranger's little demonstration, she wanted to explore that possibility right now.

Slowly, he withdrew his finger.

Lauren moaned in protest. "No. More."

She ached for that long, strong cock inside her—anywhere inside her—giving her everything, sending her into the hot burst of ecstasy only he could deliver.

"Please," she panted. "Please. I need you. To feel you…"

"You need me to fuck you?"

"Yes."

"To make love to you."

He kept coming back to this argument, and she wasn't sure why. And at the moment, she didn't care. As long as he ended her torment. "Yes. Now. Please!"

A shiver wracked her as his body covered hers, pressing her down to the table's chilled, flat surface. Her nipples beaded, tight and stunningly sensitive, as her stranger grabbed her hips and plunged inside her swollen sex in one ferocious stroke.

Lauren cried out at his invasion. In this position, her channel was smaller, and he felt enormous. And utterly perfect.

She shook as he withdrew almost all the way in a slow retreat that had her gritting her teeth. A moment later, he pushed back in with a quick thrust that ripped a gasp from her chest and sent a jolt of sensation straight to her clit.

"That's it," he crooned in her ear as he slammed her again, gripping her hips with ferocious fingers. "Now, let's make you come again."

After one more pounding stroke, Lauren stood on the tips of her toes, gasping for air. Three later, the vise of need tightened into a harsh knot under her clit, spreading unbearable heat between her legs. She reached under herself to stroke it.

"Touch yourself. That's good. I want to feel you come."

Another two strokes of his cock, and he swelled inside her, pulsing against her walls. He was on the edge, too. Lauren felt it in the bite of his fingers on her hips, his labored breathing on her neck. She tightened on him. He cursed and slammed into her one more time, scraping over her G-spot, shoving right into her cervix.

She screamed as the dam of sensation burst inside her and pleasure shocked through her system, cascading down to her fingertips and toes. As his hoarse shout erupted in her ear, a wave of dizzy rapture washed through her veins, and Lauren had to hold on to the table to steady herself.

Mr. Mysterious planted hot-breathed kisses on her shoulder and held her against him. Like the last time, she sensed his effort to bring her close, keep her beside him. It wasn't a simple post-coital thanks. It wasn't an attempt to get her ready for another round of demanding sex. The way he held her, it was like she mattered. A lot.

The possibility thrilled her...even though it shouldn't.

"God, you're amazing," he gruffed in-between harsh breaths in her ear. "No woman gets to me the way you do."

His admission surprised her. "Really?"

"Really."

She frowned. "How can that be? With your...skill, it's obvious you haven't been lacking partners."

"No, I haven't."

And yet she alone made him feel this way. Elation soared through her. Why should she be alone in this madness? Pride followed. *She* got to him. *She* made him burn.

"Why am I the only one who makes you feel this way?"

He hesitated, masking the pause by withdrawing from her body and righting his jeans. "Because my heart is in this, Lauren."

His heart? This was sounding suspiciously…heavy. Nervous, she turned, smoothed a hand down her hopelessly wrinkled skirt, then crossed her arms over her bare breasts self-consciously. "What do you mean?"

"This isn't a casual fuck for me. Surely you can feel that."

Yes, she could. Lauren's thoughts raced back over their encounters. The fact this meant something to him was evident in every touch. Each was infused with lust and longing and something more than just the momentary need to screw. She hadn't thought about it much before. But now…it gave her pause.

"What are you saying?"

He grabbed her arms, pulling her closer. "I love you."

Love? He thought he *loved* her?

She stiffened and jerked out of his grip. "No, you can't." Panic set in. "Impossible. I don't know you. You don't know me."

"Bullshit," he spit out. "We know each other, heart and body. I've watched you for years, wanted you forever. You feel it. Some part of you knows me and wants me, too, or you wouldn't respond to me with such abandon. You're going to love me."

Panic swallowed her whole. "No. I don't want to love anyone again. I'm done with love."

"You're not made to be alone for the rest of your days. I'm going to be the man who fills your life."

She shook her head, edging away from him. "Get out."

His hands bunched into fists. Shoulders tensed. He looked ready to argue as he snatched his black bag up from the floor near his feet and sent her a terse nod. "Think about what I've said because you haven't seen the last of me."

Chapter Seven

Early Tuesday morning, Noah spotted Lauren stirring her coffee. Alone and somewhat distracted. Perfect for what he had in mind.

He sidled up to her, discreetly inhaling her female, vanilla-tinged musk—and his memory transported him back to the previous night, having her spread out like a buffet across her dining room table with her ass in the air and her wet, swollen pussy completely open to him. Her little pants and cries as he toyed with her lush body, then filled her with his aching cock, had nearly destroyed his self-control. Just thinking about last night, desire roared to life, despite the fact she did nothing more enticing now than stare at the speckled Formica counter.

Not the time or place to start sweating, Reeves.

The only thing that would have made the previous night better would have been to sleep next to Lauren all night and wake up to her kiss in the morning.

Soon... He promised himself that.

"Good morning."

At the sound of his voice, she started, then sent him an embarrassed smile. "Oh, I didn't hear you come in. I was off in space somewhere. Morning."

Shelley Bradley

Weariness surrounded her eyes. They looked a bit puffy. Red and tired.

"You didn't sleep well." Noah frowned in concern.

"No."

"Something wrong?"

Lauren hesitated, like she was weighing whether she should say anything about her evening with her stranger.

"Just…a lot on my mind. You?"

Noah kept his disappointment that she didn't open up to himself. "Yeah. I didn't sleep, either."

But for an entirely different reason, he was sure.

Last night, Lauren had given him everything he'd asked for, responded so completely it had blown his mind. Certainly, a woman like her wouldn't give herself with such abandon without feeling a damn thing for her lover, right? That assumption had led him to vomit out the contents of his heart.

Mistake number one.

Noah himself should be slowly wooing her into "I love yous". Mr. Mysterious shouldn't be spewing them. Yes, he'd felt so connected to her after making love that he was sure his heart was hard-wired into hers. But he had to keep remembering her emotions. Her reluctance. Her fears. And stop being an impatient bastard.

After sleepless hours tossing and turning and wishing Lauren's soft, sweet curves were curled up beside him in slumber, he now had a refined strategy for wooing and winning the skittish, stubborn woman.

"Sorry to hear you didn't sleep well." She offered him a consoling smile, then lifted the coffee to her glossy lips and took a deep drink of her caffeinated heaven.

114

Noah smiled when she groaned. The woman loved her coffee.

She'd barely finished groaning when she said, "I came in a little early to get started on the focus groups, since we have limited time to complete them. Do you have a few minutes this morning to review some of the action items with me?"

"Sure. Meet me in my office in five?"

Lauren nodded. "Thanks."

Grabbing her cup, she disappeared around the corner, heading toward her cubicle. Noah poured his own cup and mentally reviewed his strategy as he wandered back to his office.

A few minutes later, Lauren entered, setting her files and laptop down on the little round table in the corner. "Ready?"

"Can I ask you a question first?"

She shrugged. "Sure."

Noah paced closer, leaned in, bracing his hands on the little table between them. He waited, watching as she regarded him with passing curiosity. As his stare continued, her regard changed. Awareness. Wariness. *Now* he had her attention. Now she wasn't all business. He held in a smile.

"The woman I told you about the other day at lunch, the divorcée," he began.

Lauren looked away, but not before he saw her face change. Cool. Struggling to collect. A flash of pain.

Oh, sugar… I'll kiss everything and make it better once you let me.

"What about her?"

He pretended he didn't notice how guarded her voice was. But it was damn hard to miss.

"I've been trying to tell her how I feel about her, how serious I am." He paused, waited for her to look his way again with those soulful brown eyes. "It's not going well."

She hesitated, like she was wrestling with herself. *Answer? Don't answer?* Noah understood. If she wanted to ask his advice about another man, he'd be weighing her happiness against his need. In this case, he was convinced they were the same. But if their situations were reversed and he had to watch her pine for another man...he'd be none too happy, either.

Finally, she spoke. "You really think she's going to make you happy? You've never been the sort of man for just one woman."

"I've wanted to be. I was just waiting for this woman. I need to convince her she's the one."

"But if she's been hurt, like you said..."

Noah nodded. He was pretty sure Tim had shaken Lauren's confidence as a woman and her belief in a happily-ever-after. He made a mental note to wallop his old pal upside the head next time they played poker.

"I can almost guarantee she has been."

"And how long ago was her divorce final?"

Noah tried to be vague. "At least a year."

"Still, I've been divorced for nearly two. And emotionally, the marriage was over shortly after Cass was born. If this woman has only been divorced for a year, then talk of love and marriage is too much too soon."

With a sigh, Noah sat in the chair right across from her. He'd known she would say that. He just hoped now that she'd listen to a different perspective.

"I'm trying to respect that. Honestly. But I've waited so long... It doesn't have to be a serious relationship today, and I wouldn't push so hard, except that she's shutting me out to everything but casual friendship. I do want to be her friend—but so much more." Noah closed his eyes. In no way did he have to feign his frustration, fear, and heartache. "It's tearing me up. I don't know how to coax her into compromise. I don't know how to convince her that I won't hurt her. Ever."

"You really mean all that." She sounded surprised, nearly shocked. A dawning realization peppered her tone, laced with shades of pain.

Noah gritted his teeth again, hating the fact all this fucking subterfuge was necessary. Damn the willful woman. Damn Tim for marrying her without loving her in the first place. It chapped his hide that he couldn't just grab the woman, tell her he loved her, and kiss her until she melted in his arms and agreed to stay there forever. He'd never hurt Lauren, just love her.

"I do mean it. Men don't talk about love easily, so to be thwarted so utterly is tough."

"Love?" She'd definitely morphed from surprised to shocked.

"I'm not going to marry someone I don't love."

Lauren swallowed, her face pale. But she sent him a businesslike nod, clearly trying to hide her upset. "Of course not."

"Suggestions on how to deal with this situation?"

"Well...no." She sat across from him, worrying her hands into a knot and looking anywhere but him. "I'm afraid I'm the last person you should ask. Something similar happened with me last night. I didn't handle it—"

"Mr. Mysterious?"

"He really shocked me. I handled it badly. I probably hurt his feelings. But that's different. I don't even know who he is."

"True, but given his single-minded pursuit, I'd say the guy has feelings for you." He shrugged, trying to play it casual. "I guess I'm asking what it would take for you to start looking at someone as a potential lover and mate."

She sighed. "I don't know. I haven't thought about it much. I mean, he'd have to be good with the girls. He'd have to be steady. I've got enough on my plate, so I don't need to be supporting a grown man. I'd have to feel a spark. I think that was my mistake with Tim. We married because everyone expected it and I let my mom convince me that steadiness was way more relevant than spark. This time, I'd want both."

"You know I'm steady, and I'm pretty sure we've got the spark."

Lauren chewed on her lip. Noah could tell she didn't like this conversation. Good. He didn't want her liking the thought of him with another woman. He didn't want anyone but Lauren, and the sooner she accepted the two of them together, the faster all this would end.

"Make her laugh," Lauren went on, amazing him.

She was putting what she thought were his needs above her own? That had to say something about her feelings for him…

"Laughter is good," he concurred.

"Make her feel good about herself and about being with you. Press a little, but not too hard. If the spark is really there and you truly care about her, she won't be able to resist forever."

Bless her for the straightforward answer…and the means to help him tackle her reluctant heart. "If I do all those things, do you think she'll hold out more than another few weeks?"

She sent him a lost expression with so much sadness in her eyes. Noah knew she could have no idea that her heart was written all over her face. "Knowing your persistence, your charm, and not to mention your ability to plan any situation just the way you want it, she may not last another ten minutes."

"That's exactly what I want to hear."

☙ ☙ ☙

"Kat, I've really screwed up," Lauren clutched the steering wheel of her car in one hand and the cell phone in the other, while navigating five o'clock traffic from downtown Dallas to the burbs north. "You've got to help me."

"You're not the dramatic one," Kat teased. "That's my job. So whatever you did couldn't be that bad."

"No?" she challenged. "Remember Noah Reeves?"

"Oh, yes. Yummy bachelor. Tim's buddy, right? Hey, you work for him now, don't you?"

"Yes on all counts. And I've got this…crush on him. Which is crazy. He's a total playboy, and I don't need a broken heart. I'm trying to forget it. All the while, he's asking me advice on how to get some other woman, a divorcée, to give him the time of day."

Kat whistled. "That sucks."

"Completely.

"Is he totally insensitive?"

"Not insensitive. Clueless. I've tried really hard not to let on…"

"At least I don't have to kick his balls in for being a jerk on purpose—yet."

"Listen to me. He wants to *marry* this woman. He's never *thought* the word marriage in thirty-nine years, much less said it to anyone else. The minute I get interested in him, he's all into white lace and promises with someone her."

"I'm sorry, honey... You win some, you lose some."

"Wait, it gets worse. I can't forget Noah because, in the meantime, some stranger keeps coming into my house—"

Kat gasped. "Are you okay? Did he attack you? Did you call 911?"

"He didn't attack me. I'm fine." Lauren sighed, wondering how she was going to explain this to her sister. She was supposed to be the level-headed one who bailed Kat out of scrapes, not the other way around. Damn.

"What happened?"

"He—he seduced me. It's hard to call 911 when you wake up bound to your own bed, writhing in pleasure."

"*What???*"

Lauren frowned. "That does sound bad, doesn't it? Well...whoever this guy is, he's damn good between the sheets."

"You slept with a total stranger who snuck into your house? Like, he was there to steal your DVD player but since it was broken, he just decided to nail you instead? And you let him?"

"Not like that, Kat. He said he came there for me. To be with me. To seduce me. He says he wants me and that I know him, but I can't place his voice. He whispers a lot, tries to disguise his voice by talking low and gruff."

"Are you sure you're not confusing seduction with coercion? This is not like you, and I gotta tell you, I'm worried. Really worried. I'm pretty sure the kind of guy who sneaks into a stranger's house in order

120

to 'be with her' has some sort of psychological disorder that's long, hard to pronounce, and shared by a long list of serial killers."

"It's not like that. *He's* not like that. It's…" Realizing that she was defending the very situation about which she'd come to her sister for advice, Lauren fell silent.

"He's not like that *yet*. You're lucky that, so far, he hasn't been, like, psycho lover who knows lots about knives and how to chop stupid women up into little bitty pieces."

"No. Just the opposite. Last night, he said he…loves me."

"Loves you? And you're sure this isn't the 'love you to death' kind of thing?"

"I know it sounds weird—"

"Um…yeah."

"But he's not at all threatening. Sexy, amazing, mind-blowing." Lauren sighed. "But I—I just keep picturing Noah every time he…"

"He, what? Forces you to have sex with him?"

Lauren felt herself flushing hot. "He doesn't have to force me."

"Oh my… Unbelievable. You're screwed in the head and every which way. You're usually the practical one, but I'm going to give you the advice for a change."

"No more berating?"

"No. It won't do any good anyway."

"Good. I need help. I'm tied up in so many knots, I can't figure out what to do."

"First, you've got to stop sleeping with someone you don't know. Next time he comes over, demand to know who he is or tell him to get the hell out."

"I've asked who he is…" she protested.

But she hadn't demanded. Or threatened to scream the walls down or withhold her response if he didn't reveal himself. With a guilty pang, she remembered that, last night, she hadn't even wanted to know who he was for sure. Because whoever he was…he wasn't Noah. And as long as she didn't know his real identity, she could pretend.

"Ask again," Kat ground out. "Before he does his Norman Bates impression. Are the girls at the house when all this is—"

"No. They've been with Tim or Mom."

"Good. *Demand* to know who he is. Then demand that he leaves and tries to date you like a normal person."

"It wouldn't matter if Mr. Mysterious did. I don't want anyone but Noah. And he's…in love with someone else." Lauren paused, gripping the phone. "I'm afraid, Kat."

"Buck up, sweetie. It's simple, not scary. You're going to tell the night stalker to get lost. Tell him you want someone else. That usually sends a guy flying in the other direction unless he's some sort of emotional masochist."

Nodding, Lauren conceded the point. "True, but Noah is into this other woman. Once he catches her, and he will, then I'll be alone again."

"Let me get this straight. You'd rather be with some guy who sneaks into your house and tells you he loves you, even if you don't know or love him back?"

Damn, when had Kat gotten so logical? "No. You're right."

"For a change, I am. And if you want Noah for yourself, you need to make a move before this bitch gets her claws in him. See if he feels anything for you before he gets too tangled up in this other woman."

"Make a move, how? Like walk up to him and tell him I fantasize about him? He's talking about marriage and babies with this woman. He wants to settle down. I was thinking more...fling."

"Until this other woman says 'I do,' Noah is still an unattached man. Honey, if he's got hormones, he'll do fling."

"Maybe it's not smart. He's my boss and Tim's buddy. Maybe I should just get over it."

"I know you. You're not going to just get over it. And maybe it's good you start dating or flinging or something again. Hell, prior to this brain blip, you'd lived like a nun since the divorce," Kat pointed out. "Look, the boss-buddy thing you'll have to work around. Don't bring it up at the office. Don't mention Tim. But if Noah rebuffs you, at least you'll know, right? If he doesn't...could be a hot night for my slightly older and uglier sister."

At their running joke about which of the sisters was the uglier, Lauren snorted. "Yeah, uglier? Who went dateless on prom night? Not me..."

"Ugh! Always the same argument. Rub in it, why don't you? Hey, at least I'm not so sex-starved that I'm letting some horny cat burglar in my panties."

"That's low. I won't let him in my panties again."

"You see the wisdom of genius Kat's advice, do you?"

"Genius is a bit thick, but yeah. I think so."

"Go get rid of the psycho and bag your man, tigress."

Tigress? At the moment, she felt like a whipped, wet kitten. That wasn't any way to get Noah to notice her as a woman. But the reality of Kat's advice was sinking in. She had to make a pass at Noah. Oh, yikes! Lauren grimaced. The very thought made her palms sweat and her stomach turn with nerves. "I'm, um...on it."

"You don't sound on it; you sound reluctant."

Her sister was so perceptive sometimes. "Noah invited the girls and I over for a swim and a barbeque on Thursday evening. What should I do?"

"Really?" Kat sounded as if that was a vastly interesting fact. "Has he ever done that before?"

Lauren thought, then frowned. "No."

"Interesting… Very interesting, in fact. Okay, let's talk strategy. I have ideas…"

Chapter Eight

On Wednesday night, Lauren sagged into her Jacuzzi tub, glass of wine in one hand, and enjoyed the relaxing vanilla sugar bath salts. The candle sat on the counter near the door, flame bobbing as it burned, adding a golden sliver of light.

Well, she would be enjoying it if she could take her mind off Noah. And Mr. Mysterious. And her conversation with Kat.

And the mess her life had become.

At least, nothing was wrong with the girls, thank goodness. Her mother had wanted to keep them another day, which enabled Lauren to finish up a report at work so the focus groups could move forward. The extra time at the office had settled that part of her life. But now…with night descended and the loneliness creeping in, she didn't want to be by herself.

That wasn't accurate. Not for anything would she take Tim back. The idea of a bar and the kind of guy she might meet there left her cold. She wanted Noah, fiercely—but not when he wanted someone else.

To add to her confusion, sultry nights like this one made her body call for—crave—what Mr. Mysterious could give her. She'd promised Kat that she'd tell the stranger to take a hike, and if he appeared tonight, she'd do her best to keep that promise. But everything about him, from the way he mastered her body, to the hard feel of him all over, and the tangy-salt taste of his skin, was pure fantasy. Add her unruly imagination to the mix, the one that encouraged her to imprint Noah's face on Mr. Mysterious's body and...well, it was a good thing he hadn't appeared last night. Or so far tonight. She felt vulnerable.

Weak.

And Lord knew, her stranger's charm was potent.

Eyes closed, Lauren lifted the wine to her lips and finished off the last swallow of the dry, fruity blend.

In mid-swallow, she heard a creak, followed by a puff of air. By the time she opened her eyes, it was pitch black in the windowless bathroom. She set aside the glass and thrust back the curtain. The bathroom door was closed and the candle extinguished. No way could she see a thing.

Lauren gasped.

Her stranger was here. Suddenly, she knew it. She felt him in the air that vibrated, burned, between them. Her heart revved up like an F-22's engine, ready to soar out of her chest. Her mind buzzed. What should she do? She couldn't climb out of the tub and get past him in the narrow room without him knowing. But she couldn't just surrender—no matter how appealing that choice sounded.

She was fucked, figuratively and literally.

"Lauren."

His voice, that lust-gruff whisper. Mr. Mysterious. She exhaled, shaky, anxious...even as she felt parts south go all warm and wet at the very thought of his touch. Wetter still as she imagined Noah sneaking into her bathroom to touch her, have his wicked way with her.

"You scared me." Her voice shook.

"You should know it's me. You should know I can't stay away from you for more than a night now that I know how perfectly you grip my cock. I need to fuck you too bad to stay away."

His words would have melted her panties if she'd been wearing any. But what about the way she'd rebuffed his declaration of love? She didn't know much about this man, but she doubted he'd just decided to forget that little incident.

The rustle of cloth, the rasp of a zipper, the whooshing sound of denim hitting the floor. *Oh my God.* He was getting undressed.

"No. Don't get naked. Don't come any closer."

"Too late," he growled as he stepped into the tub, a foot on either side of her hips, then sank to his knees and covered her body with every hard inch of his own.

Sweet and forbidden as he hovered over her, all harsh breaths and tense need. Such a perfect fit. Feeling him against her did something to her. Not just her arousal, though she couldn't deny hers was escalating faster than the price of oil. But her heart gave an unpleasant little thump at the thought of denying him.

But she had to stop this. "We can't—"

"You made yourself perfectly clear on Monday night. No love. Fine. Don't keep your body from me. Just spread your legs and let me do everything I want to that sweet pussy…"

No. The word was on the tip of her tongue…but she swallowed it when Mr. Mysterious whispered his wicked request against her mouth, then his lips crashed over hers, tongue urging her to open for him so he could ravage her with a ruthless kiss.

Wet, aggressive, he kissed her with scorching skill. Sinking into her mouth, farther with each pass of his lips, the kiss felt like he intended to brand her with his possession. He mated with her tongue, and she adopted his rhythm, arched toward him, burned for more. The feel of him amazed her, perfect and male, hungry and demanding, confident and determined. She could totally picture Noah behaving like this with a woman…and the fantasies of him here with her in the bathtub weren't something she could stop. Or wanted to stop.

The insistent press of his lips smothering the little whimpers that escaped her throat echoed around them. Lauren raised her arms to clutch him. Blessedly bare. Bare back, hard and rippling with muscle when he moved. Bare, bulging shoulders so wide they nearly spanned the width of the tub. Bare face and head, devoid of a mask she noticed as she sank her fingers into his collar-length hair to feel the silky strands with just a hint of wave.

She could absolutely picture Noah here with her now. And she did, throwing herself into the kiss with all the frustrated need he roused that coursed through her.

"That's it. Let me have your mouth, too. I need it. Then I'll fuck you so hard and long until you come all over my cock. I'm going to make sure you know who that pussy responds to."

Lauren whimpered again. Any other man she would suspect of bragging. Mr. Mysterious… If anyone could do as promised, it was him.

But wasn't she supposed to be saying no? Resisting? Yes, but why? The answer totally eluded her as he pinched suddenly tender nipples—and every nerve ending in her breasts remembered his rough, pleasure-inducing treatment from Monday night. They applauded the pinch and roll his fingers bestowed on the hard tips. Before she could stop herself, Lauren arched toward him for more.

Warm water sloshed around them as he readjusted himself, climbing higher up her torso and grabbing her head with a desperate grip. "I need your mouth now. Suck me."

Then he was palming the back of her head with one hand and guiding his cock to her mouth with the other.

Lauren frowned. She didn't want this. She didn't. Oral sex was too intimate. She didn't know him. Taking him into her mouth and pleasuring him would only make him more insistent that she belonged with him, to him. The intimacy of the act might make the foolish woman inside her think the same thing. She couldn't risk it.

And yet, when the swollen velvety head of his cock brushed her lips, she opened, unable to resist just a taste. Salty, male, tantalizing. Knowing she could make him leak before she'd even touched him gave her a little thrill.

After a shy flick of her tongue, a long groan spilled from his chest. Lauren relished the sound way more than she ought to. His fingers tightened in her hair, urging her to take more of him, to establish a rhythm with speed and sizzle.

As she wrapped her tongue around the head on the next upstroke, he hissed and cursed and fucked her mouth as if he'd never get enough.

"Yes," he groaned. "Damn, that's good… Suck me, sugar."

Sugar. He'd called her sugar again. Just like Noah. Not totally uncommon for southern men, and she did hear a bit of Texas in some of his growled words. But that wasn't odd here in Dallas.

Did you hear Noah in his voice because you wish so badly that he was Mr. Mysterious?

If she was honest with herself, likely yes. But with Noah panting after Divorcée Barbie, talking babies and marriage, the chances of him being in her home, in her tub—hell, in her mouth—moaning and clasping her hair in his fists—that was pretty slim.

Lauren pushed the thoughts from her mind. She couldn't smell anything—weird defect in her genetic make up—but she could absolutely taste her Mr. Mysterious. Clean skin, a hint of salt and musk and male that drove her completely wild.

She reached up to cup his testicles, which felt round and heavy as they lay in her palm. They drew up as she slicked her tongue up his shaft and curled over the sensitive head again, this time giving him a gentle nip of her teeth.

Mysterious hissed. "You're flirting with danger now. Keep that up and you'll stay there until you suck me dry."

Crazy and wild, but his words sent a thrill through her. The thought of having the power and finesse necessary to bring this man to his knees—literally—ramped her up dangerously fast. Her breasts hung heavy, ached. Her sex clamped down with a hungry clench of need. She slipped a hand between her legs and fumbled around for her clit.

The sloshing water must have alerted him. Or was it her whimper when her fingers first made contact with the hard knot of need?

"You touching yourself?" At her nod, he panted, "Oh, yeah. That's it. Come with me."

Rubbing furiously at her clit, Lauren's need skyrocketed within seconds. Blood rushed through her body, heart pumping. Her stranger filled her mouth, leaking more fluid. Urgency flowed from his fingertips and his touch deep into her. She sucked harder, faster. He cursed and groaned, hardened again and pulsed on her tongue. He was seconds away, and desire clawed at her. She wanted this. For some reason, in that moment, she needed to know that she could send him into bliss the way he could do to her.

"Lauren." He barely got her name out between harsh breaths. "Ready?"

She moaned, dragging her fingertip over the swollen bud of nerves screaming to explode.

Seconds later, it did. She did, saturating her body with the white heat of lightning pleasure. He joined her, flooding her mouth with the salty taste of him, filling her ears with his ragged groans and a torn curse.

Triumph and elation swirled with an encroaching oh-shit feeling. What had she done? Now she knew the taste of him and she'd want it again. She was supposed to be discouraging the man, sending him away. Somehow she didn't think that sucking him to an orgasm so hard he was still trying to find his breath was going to give him the "get lost" message.

"You shouldn't be here," she finally uttered.

Above her, his body tensed. "Because you don't love me?"

"Because I don't know you. This is insane! You keep sneaking into my house—"

"And you keep letting me into your bed, your body. Obviously, I'm not the only one out of my mind."

"Oh, I agree. My behavior is completely mental. This needs to stop."

He eased away, stood. The tub started to drain.

"Easy to say that after the orgasm, isn't it?" he taunted. "Don't make something out of nothing. You want to fuck and that's it. I get it. I can be accommodating."

No doubt, he could be extremely accommodating. But she still heard the anger in his voice. Nothing good could come from this.

"This isn't a good idea," she said gently.

"Having your own secret fuck toy isn't a good idea? Just think, no maintenance. Nothing to share except your pussy and your mouth…and your ass, if you'll let me have it. No messy emotions or commitments. No man's dirty underwear to pick up off the floor. No one to hog the remote control. No guy to hear snoring at night. Perfect, isn't it?"

No one to hold her as she drifted off to sleep. No man to soothe her when it had been a hard day. No helpmate to care about, to turn to in tough times.

God, he was messing with her head. With her heart. Despite the fact the tub was nearly empty and the air was cold on her wet skin, Lauren drew her knees up to her chest. Hot tears scalded the backs of her eyes, her cheeks.

"What do you want?" she sobbed.

He didn't reply, but bent and lifted her against his body. Lauren put her arms around him, anticipating the tender warmth of his embrace.

Instead, he laid her out on the soft area rug stretched across her bathroom floor, covered her body with his, and filled her with his cock in one hard thrust.

"I want to give you what you're after. A good fuck. Another orgasm."

The grip of his fingers on her hips conveyed the hint of anger that haunted his voice. His words hurt her. And yet…she couldn't stop her body from resisting. After a handful of times inside her, Mysterious already knew how to wring the most reaction from her with every quick lunge of his hips and torturously slow withdrawal.

Friction, heat, desire all clawed at her. But there was more. Lauren lifted her hips in welcome, threw her arms around him and kissed the hard line of his jaw in atonement. Her affection had no effect on him. He continued to pound away at her, lifting her from the rug with each ferocious thrust into her body.

"Don't be angry," she managed to get out, though finding coherent words not lost in a sea of pleasure was damned difficult.

"I'm not angry. I'm aroused."

Lauren didn't believe him, but he robbed her of the ability to protest when he rolled one nipple between his thumb and forefinger. Pleasure shot straight from the sensitive tip all the way down to her sex, which clenched in hunger. He growled and repeated the action.

God, she was getting wetter by the moment. Hotter. The man could drive her to the brink of sanity in minutes. She'd never reacted to Tim or any other man this strongly—ever. It was exhilarating. It was scary as hell.

She couldn't catch a breath, couldn't stop herself from responding to him, couldn't prevent the burn from racing through her body and setting her blood on fire. She couldn't keep from wrapping her legs around his hips and inviting him deeper. And when his palm skated down her side, over the curve of her hip and settled between their bodies, Lauren couldn't hold in her whimper.

Before she could even catch a breath, he trapped her clit between his fingers, gave her a gentle pinch, and plunged his cock in to the hilt. "C'mon, Lauren. Come for me. Come!"

At the pleasure-pain of his touch and his growled command, Lauren obeyed, exploding in sharp shards of light and heat and colors. She dug her nails into his back as she clamped down on his cock, milking him, igniting every nerve ending she'd ever felt—and a few she hadn't known existed.

Then he pulsed, stiffened, roared...and joined her in pleasure.

They shared ragged breaths and racing hearts and tangled limbs. And Lauren couldn't deny a tug toward the man. He moved her body, without question. And he'd admitted to loving her. Why? She had no idea who he was. And she'd used him for her pleasure. Granted, he'd taken some too, but not happily. The anger in his voice, in his touch, was clear. Guilt tugged at her.

Tonight, she'd meant to say no. To tell him to leave and not come back. A pair of mind-boggling orgasms later...it was too late.

Shame burned, even as the desire to touch him grew. And why? She'd dubbed him Noah in her mind and she didn't want to know why. She'd given herself to him completely—again.

Now, she was going to have to pay the price by putting an end to this. It wasn't fair to take pleasure from one man while thinking of another.

Her conversation with Kat came rushing back. *Fine time...* Now she recalled. She was supposed to tell Mysterious that she wanted someone else. But gee, after sucking him off and then spreading her legs for him so submissively on the bathroom floor, what were the odds that he'd believe her?

Lauren sighed, screwed up her courage, and opened her mouth to hopefully say the right thing to let him down without hurting him. Instead, he withdrew from her body and stood in one fluid motion. Suddenly, she felt cold.

The rustle of clothing told her he was dressing.

Lauren frowned. "You're leaving?"

He stilled. "You ready for another round?"

Yes. No. Hell, she was confused. What did she want? Lauren searched herself... This was bad. She just wanted him to touch her, hold her. In his arms she felt desirable and sexy, like she imagined a woman in Noah Reeves's bed would feel.

But she wanted him to actually *be* Noah. It wasn't going to happen.

"I didn't think so," he muttered.

"You're just going to go?" she blurted.

A moment later, he grabbed her wrist and looped something around it, then dragged her arm upward. He'd affixed her to her own towel bar. Before she could cuss at him, he snapped a blindfold over her eyes.

"Yep. I offered you more last time. Everything. You made yourself clear. Sex. Just sex. I got the message. You got fucked. I'll see you next time I have an itch to scratch."

His words horrified her. "You son of a bitch. That's low. That's lower than low. I never meant—"

The slam of the door cut her off. He was gone. He really had just…got up and left.

Lauren sat stunned. Even if she could have uncuffed her wrist in time to catch him, she wouldn't have moved. Couldn't have. She felt weirdly empty. And ashamed. God, what had she done?

On numb legs, she stood and plucked off the blindfold, then leaned over and flipped on the light switch. The face that confronted her in the mirror dismayed her. Flushed and disheveled, lips swollen, hair a ratted mess. She looked like a woman who'd been fucked. Not well loved. Just…used. The way she'd used him.

A fresh wave of guilt assailed her.

Quickly, she untied the loose knot around her wrist and stumbled to her bed as fresh, hot tears burned paths down her cheeks.

CR CR CR

Noah damn near jumped out of his skin when the doorbell rang.

Lauren had arrived. She would be here, under this roof. Finally.

The day had dragged on interminably. Staring at Lauren, her hair falling softly over her shoulders, from across a conference room table hadn't been good for his concentration this afternoon. Remembering the feel of her hot and tight around him while he plunged as far into her as possible and wishing he could merge with her forever hadn't been productive when discussing the business's bottom line and possible expansion plans. Wondering what she'd thought of Mr. Mysterious's impersonal late-night screw in her bathroom had worn his nerves thin.

Earlier today, he'd arranged for the delivery of a collection of erotic vignettes from Mr. Mysterious to her, at her house, with certain passages marked, scenarios that were a bit rough, male dominating, sometimes crude. He'd included a note that simply read, *Next time I have an itch to scratch...* No signature. Had she opened the package, scanned the stories he'd flagged?

It had bothered him like hell to treat her that way, to treat her worse than the dozens of women he'd nailed and forgotten in his past. The confusion and hurt in her voice had torn at him. The way she'd clung to him as he'd risen to dress had nearly caused him to lose his resolve. But he'd held firm, reminded himself that the end justified the means. He had a point to make. And he was close, damn close, to his prize.

Focus.

Now it was time to push last night, today at the office, and everything else aside. At this moment, he wasn't her boss, or Mr.

Mysterious. Now he could just be himself and do his best to gently romance her—enough that she'd start getting the picture, but not so much that she'd run screaming. All the games and subterfuge would end soon.

Noah hoped like hell that he could finally make love to her as himself.

He smiled as he answered the door.

On the other side, Lauren stood with Emma on one side, Cass on her hip, looking spring fresh and scrumptious with a gauzy cover-up that didn't totally hide her slinky black bathing suit and luscious body underneath. His mouth watered. Other parts were dangerously close to standing at attention in a very visible way.

"Hi, Lauren, girls. Come in," he invited.

As they filed inside, Emma sent him a very solemn look for a six-year-old. He wondered what it would take to make the girl smile again. Of everyone affected, the divorce had hit this child the hardest. She reminded him of Tim—all drive, buried sense of humor, and damn smart. Still, he hoped that she gave herself the chance to be a little girl before it was too late. And he hoped he could help her.

"Thank you for inviting us," Emma said without a smile.

"You're welcome. I haven't used my pool that much since I moved in. It's getting lonely, so I *had* to invite some company over."

Emma frowned. "Pools don't get lonely. They get dirty."

Too serious by far. Over time, he'd find a way to put a smile back on her face.

"Are you sure? I could swear I heard it whispering to me... 'Why bother if you never use me?'"

A corner of Emma's little pink mouth twitched. "You're silly."

"Twim. Now!" Cass demanded, wriggling on Lauren's hip until the child nearly fell.

Noah scooped the little blonde bundle up with a laugh and a hug.

"Right now," Noah promised.

"Sorry," Lauren murmured. "They're a handful."

"They're wonderful. This big ol' house has been way too silent lately. We all could use a good time."

"It's a huge house for one," she said, looking around.

Noah shrugged. Better not to mention just now that, about a year ago, he'd purchased this four bedroom, three bath house with her and the girls in mind...and made sure the place had enough room for a nursery.

"Lots of room is never a bad thing," he said vaguely. "Good tax break."

He noticed then that Lauren carried a large bag over her shoulder stuffed with towels and other goodies. It smelled of...

"Chocolate chip cookies?" His nose wasn't deceiving him, right?

Lauren made the best cookies. After one bite, if he hadn't already fallen in love with her, he'd have surrendered his heart on the spot.

"Emma and I baked a quick batch as a thank you for inviting us."

"Walnuts?" he asked hopefully.

"Some with, some without. Cass is allergic to most nuts."

Noah made a mental note to be careful with the little girl and nuts as he led them deeper into the house, past the formal living and dining rooms, to the kitchen and the back of the house. Emma hovered close to a corner, while Cass ran across the floor and pressed her face against the French doors, looking out at the pool beyond.

Lauren set her bag down and regarded him with a self-conscious expression. "What can I do to help with dinner?"

"Just talk to me. Everything is mostly ready. All I have to do is barbeque." He turned back to the girls. "Who wants hamburgers and hot dogs?"

"Me!" Cass bounced up and down.

"Yes, please," Emma said quietly, clutching a Junie B. Jones book in her little hands.

"Maybe you can have one of each and we won't tell your mom," he said in a stage whisper.

"I heard that." Lauren smiled.

"Darn." Noah laughed. "I suppose I'll have to let you punish me later," he shot her a wicked grin…just to watch her reaction.

Lauren didn't disappoint. She flushed a sweet rosy shade. "You wish."

She had no idea. If the punishment included some reciprocal action, he was definitely all for it.

ଔ ଔ ଔ

Within a few minutes, Lauren followed Noah outside and chatted as he grilled their dinner. A few potato chips and some fruit salad later, they were eating. Afterward, the girls swam. Cass paddled with her floaties, laughing. Emma rigorously practiced her freestyle up and down the pool until Lauren had to remind her that swimming was supposed to be fun, too.

She sighed.

"You're worried about her." Noah glanced across the small patio at Emma.

Twilight wrapped them in a warm-breezed cocoon, decorated with twinkling lights and emerging stars. How romantic it was here, among his wild plants and tropical flowers, the pool's waterfall gently rushing in the background. The girls played quietly and, for a moment, she could imagine that she and Noah were alone.

Dangerous. Stupid. Asking for a broken heart.

Unavoidable.

"Yes," she said finally. "I worry about Emma. She's so…"

"Like Tim. Very serious. You're doing the right things to encourage her to be a kid while she can."

"I know. She just has so little to be happy about. Kids tease her for being so smart. I try to be both Mom and Dad but—"

"It's not the same as having a father for her, is it?"

"No. I had such a special bond with my dad before he passed away. It kills me that Em and Cass don't have the same thing."

"Maybe you'll remarry someday."

She rolled her eyes. "I've been married and done that. Thanks, but no."

"Never say never."

Noah looked at her then, straight at her, deep in her eyes. His pale blue eyes sizzled with something, and Lauren's heart skipped a beat. Why did he care if she remarried?

She stared back, focusing for a moment on his hair, which fell just to his collar, waving slightly as it brushed his forehead and ears. His mouth snared her gaze next, followed by the width of his shoulders. Familiarity tugged at her, not because he seemed like himself in that moment. But as darkness descended and shadows enveloped the yard, he reminded her of Mr. Mysterious. Different voice, but so many other things were so similar.

No. Impossible. Stupid, wishful thinking.

"Mom, can I have a cookie now?" Emma asked, wrapped in a big orange beach towel.

"Sure, they're in the house. Take Cass with you and give her one, too. Dry off and sit at the kitchen table. No wet feet on Noah's carpet."

"Yes, ma'am." Emma took her little sister's hand and took the instructions to heart.

"Wait," Noah said softly to Emma. "You're six now?"

"Almost seven." She thrust up her little chin.

"Did you know that almost-seven-year-old girls are magical?" he asked solemnly.

Emma hesitated, her wet brown curls draped over her shoulders. "What do you mean? There's no such thing."

"There is. Girls your age, they have magic, usually in their ears. Can I look in yours?"

An even longer pause this time, still looking skeptical. "I guess. It won't hurt, will it?"

"Not a bit. Close your eyes."

For another moment, Emma paused, then she complied, her little lashes fluttering down onto rosy cheeks.

Lauren's heart clenched with sadness. Since the divorce, Emma was so afraid and mistrusting. She seemed sure that everything good would be taken away from her. She didn't want to be babied, as if she'd decided that she'd never let herself down, but everyone else might.

Noah lifted his hand and swept it behind her ear. When it emerged again, and Emma opened her eyes, there was a twinkling light between his fingers, winking right up at her older daughter.

And miracle of miracles, Emma smiled. "How'd you do that?"

"I didn't do anything. It was your magic," he assured her.

"I didn't know I was magical." The idea seemed to excite her.

"There should always be magic when you're young, before you have grown-up responsibilities and jobs. Enjoy your magic, Emma."

Her daughter cocked her head and regarded Noah with a considering expression. A little smile emerged. "I like being magical."

"How much magic you let into your life is up to you."

Emma stayed still, saying and doing nothing for a long minute. Finally, she put her cold little hand on Noah's forearm and leaned in to kiss his cheek. "Thank you."

A heartbeat later, she skipped away.

Lauren's breath caught. Tears stung her eyes. "How did you do that?"

He shrugged. "She's had so much reality in her young life, I figured she could do with a little whimsy."

"You're right. I should have tried something like that…" She smiled at him, eyes watering. "You planned that, didn't you? Just to put a smile on her face."

Of course he did. He planned *everything*.

He nodded sheepishly, confirming her suspicions. "It's no big deal…"

But it was. To her, it was a huge deal.

"You've had too much reality, too," he said, taking her hand and sliding it against his strong palm.

At his touch, her heart stuttered, then began to slam against her chest in pounding beats.

"In some ways, Emma reminds me of you," he said quietly. "She's watched you and learned about not letting anyone close, about shutting people out of your heart. Lauren, you're too young to be alone."

Wow, this conversation had turned personal—fast. She looked down, suddenly uncomfortable. "I'm not alone. I have the girls—"

"I meant a man."

Who? She wanted Noah, while he wanted some bimbo she'd never met. Mr. Mysterious wanted her, and while some part of her was attached to him, she knew she wasn't going to be happy with just sex. Last night had proven that in ugly, garish color. She wasn't going to be happy without the whole package, great sex *and* sublime happiness with a man who could make her think, make her laugh, who cared about her daughters, worked hard, played hard.

A man like Noah.

Suddenly Lauren and Noah were alone on the moon-drenched patio. He was holding her trembling hand between his strong palms, looking right into her eyes. And she was feeling decidedly nervous. And mushy right in the middle of her chest. She yearned to lean in, kiss him.

Oh, God. Noah. She...loved him.

Lauren shut her eyes, wishing she could shut out the reality that she loved the man who would be perfect for her, if only he could love her, too.

But it wasn't meant to be.

Slowly, her gaze wound back up to his. "We talked about this."

"You said a lot of bullshit I don't believe."

"It's just not going to work. But don't worry about me. How's it going with your divorcée?"

"Still up in the air. Don't change the subject. You can't be alone the rest of your life. What will you do for companionship?"

"I—I have friends. You're my friend," she pointed out.

The observation made his lips press into a thin line. He looked decidedly unhappy. "Who will help you raise the girls?"

"Plenty of other moms do it alone. I'll manage."

That answer didn't make him any happier. "What will you do for sex?"

The question took Lauren aback. She tried to snatch her hand from Noah's grip.

He held tight. "Come on, Lauren. Who is going to hold you late at night when you're tired of being alone and your body is aching? Or you've had a rough day and need someone to talk to?"

She swallowed, trying not to let the tears threatening fall. Honestly, she'd asked herself those questions before. Hundreds of times. "I don't know."

Noah cupped her cheek in his palm, his gaze intense but unreadable. Warmth seeped into her. God, what she wouldn't give to have him look at her in love and desire…and the million other emotions he'd never feel for her.

She loved him. And he'd never love her. Period. Yes, she told Kat that she would tell Noah how she felt about him, but what was the point now that he was determined to marry someone else? Right now, he had the perfect opportunity to kiss her, if he was so inclined. But he didn't…and she knew he wasn't. That spoke volumes.

"You need to start thinking about your possibilities," he said quietly.

Possibilities? Like who? Gary in Accounting, the miniature carbon copy of Tim? The new neighbor down the street who had to be fifteen years older than her? She wanted badly to confront Noah, to ask him who the hell he meant, if he was offering up himself.

But she didn't have the courage to ask or to confess what was in her heart.

For the second night in a row, she was angry with herself. Ashamed.

"It's late. The girls have school tomorrow. We'd better go."

Chapter Nine

Déjà vu. That's what trekking through Lauren's house, guided only by the flicking light of the nearly-silent TV, felt like to Noah.

Only this time he had so much more to lose.

Last night by his pool, something on Lauren's face had changed. Her resolve to stay removed from him had slipped. Besides her flushed cheeks, he'd seen tears swimming in her big brown eyes. And the way she'd looked at him in those moments, as if she could barely keep herself from touching him and blurting out whatever was in her heart.

But she'd stayed silent, damn it, forcing him to plot his next move—only he wasn't quite sure now what move to make. He, who was *never* without a plan, was suddenly forced to wing it.

Noah held in a curse as he crept down the hall, toward her bedroom, aware that winging it wasn't his strong suit and everything could blow up in his face.

But something had to give. Hours with Lauren at the office were now the most painful torture. He knew he was close to everything he wanted, close to persuading her there could be a *them*. But after ten years of waiting, he was beyond impatient.

Still, he had cause for hope. Her daughters responded to him, which was important to her. Lauren had acknowledged—even if to herself—that she wasn't going to be happy alone. They were good together, personally, professionally.

Sexually.

God, yes. Memories of her were enough to make him hard as steel. Sinking into her and drowning sounded like heaven. He cared about her. Hell, he loved her, more now than ever.

The question was, how to tell her that without scaring her away?

Wearing his black ski mask, he entered her darkened bedroom. Lauren lay on her side wearing a pale, thin tank top and little white cotton panties. He smiled. She'd said she was more than a white cotton woman when he'd sent her the red thong. He'd suspected she had a drawer full of white cotton—and he didn't care. She could wear a potato sack as long as she was his.

Easing his way to the bed, he removed the cuffs from the pocket of his jeans, intending to bind Lauren to the headboard. He couldn't just fuck her again the way he had Wednesday night. Yeah, it had felt just fine while he was balls deep inside her. But the catch in her voice and the tears he'd heard her shed after she believed he'd gone…they tore him up. But Mr. Mysterious couldn't tell her he loved her again. Noah had to be the one to say it this time.

Hell, he wished creating Mr. Mysterious had never been necessary, but he'd known he couldn't talk her into love. He had to show her what she was giving up, how good they could be, how unsatisfying "just sex" was.

Since Tim had thankfully taken the kids again for the weekend, Noah had cooked up Mr. Mysterious one more time. And he hoped this would be the last time he came to Lauren in disguise.

When he reached the side of the bed, his heart pounded. Damn, he was hard and hot and ready. But he needed to keep his cool.

Taking a deep breath, he clasped Lauren's wrist in his grip, she surprised him by jerking away from him and rolling to face him.

She was wide awake.

"I had a feeling you'd be back tonight."

Shock stupefied him. She'd expected him? What the hell was he supposed to say to that? No clue. But her hostile, challenging expression jolted Noah right out of his silence.

"Why?" He deepened his voice, changing it until it scratched even his own ears.

"You're getting predictable. You were here Monday and Wednesday…and now it's Friday. Your pattern was easy to figure out, and you always seem to know when my children are gone."

"I pay attention. Apparently, so do you."

"Why are you here? Got an itch?" she said snidely. "I'm done scratching you."

"You didn't like being treated that way?"

"Like a meaningless one-night stand. Hell no!"

"Neither did I."

Some of the anger drained from her face. She unclenched her fists. "I never meant to hurt you when you said you loved me. I panicked and I wasn't…nice."

He shrugged, wondering where this was going. "The way I approached you wasn't nice."

She sat up, then got to her knees, edging closer. "Who are you?"

"We'll get to that later."

"Now. Or I'm going to call the cops."

"No, you're not. Because then you'd have to admit that you let me in before and willingly had sex with me—repeatedly. What are the chances they'd do much to help you then?"

She set her jaw in a mutinous, tight line. "Fine. But you should know that I realized you're using the spare key on my front porch to let yourself in. After tonight, I'm moving it."

"That won't stop me. I'll pursue you until I get what I want."

"What is that exactly? If you wanted to have sex with me, you did. As you pointed out, more than once. What the hell else do you want?"

Marriage. Babies. Love. "More than a fuck."

Lauren edged away and cursed. "That's not a whole answer, and I'm done playing your games."

"Good. I'm tired of having to play them." Noah leaned closer, invading her personal space. "I can think of a lot of things I want to do with a beautiful woman like you, and playing mind games is at the bottom of the list. Touching you…" He skated a fingertip across her nearly-bare shoulder. "That's at the top."

She opened her mouth to protest, Noah was sure. Before she could, he cupped the back of her head in his palm and captured her parted lips. They were damp under his, the bottom lip slightly swollen like she'd been chewing on it again. Lauren had eaten something chocolate recently and she tasted like heaven. And hesitation. In fact, she braced her hands against his shoulders as if she meant to push him away.

Now that he had her flavor on his lips, he wouldn't let that happen.

Noah wrapped his arms around her and jerked her beneath him, then followed her body down onto the mattress with his own. She gasped, and he took advantage of her open mouth to steal inside.

Wrapping his fists in her hair, he sank past her lips, deep into the sugary-warm flavor of her, then he retreated, teasing, until Lauren sought him with her swollen lips, eager tongue, and soft little moans. He pulled back again, and she followed, coming closer, before Noah plunged back into her mouth, deeper than ever before.

With a dance and a slide, their tongues tangled, mated—just like their breaths and heartbeats. Lauren moaned, her body going pliant under him.

God, she was like utopia. Holding her, touching her, filled him with a sweet ache, even as she inflamed him.

More. More now. He had to have her.

Gliding his palms down the soft length of her curves, he reveled in a handful of her breast, the indented sweep of her waist, the lush jut of her hip, until he took her thigh in his palm and lifted it over his hip. With a moan, he slid into the cradle between her legs and notched his cock right against her. Damp, humid, welcoming. Oh…hell yes. Noah clutched at her hip, rocked against her again, rejoicing as she moaned into his mouth.

He stared down at her as silvery moonlight spilled into the room. A goddess, lush and drowning in pleasure, she looked beautiful. Her brownish-blonde hair lay in a tangle across her pillow. The red lips he ached to taste again were slightly parted as the moonbeams danced across her wonderful, familiar face. Through her tank top, her nipples stood up, their dark shadows visible through the pale cotton. His mouth watered. His cock hardened even more.

The tank top had to go.

Gripping the thin, soft garment in his fists, he gave a massive yank. Lauren gasped as it ripped right down the middle, exposing the enticing mounds of her breasts. And, oh yeah, those swollen dark nipples.

"What are you doing?" she asked.

"Taking it off would have taken too long," he growled. "I can't wait."

Patience gone, the sight of her breasts taunted his self-control. He sank down against her, arms pinning her to the bed while he feasted on the hard points of her nipples and the soft swells of flesh all around.

Her taste was hers alone. Soft female, a hint of something sugary and addicting. She smelled of vanilla and her arousal, and she was driving him out of his mind.

The more he had of her, the more he wanted. Not that he'd expected differently. He'd never wanted a woman the way he wanted Lauren. For ten years. Picturing her face as he screwed countless others. Aching just to talk to her night after night in his solitary bed. But nothing, no one, had ever come close to the reality.

Impatience chafed him. He'd waited and hidden and pretended for so long. No more. He couldn't take it another minute. He wanted to get inside her, deep, stroke her, fill her—and have her know exactly who was driving her to orgasm.

Now.

Reckless determination drove him, especially when her fingers threaded under his mask, through his hair, and he took her other nipple in his mouth. She arched to him, not just inviting, but offering, stabbing the sensitive tip against his tongue.

It was time. It had to be. Ten years of torture had to end.

His pulse damn near raced out of his chest at the thought that he could be inside her, to the hilt, bare skin to skin, looking deep into Lauren's eyes as his name fell from her lips.

"No!" she said suddenly, pushing at him.

Stunned, he lifted his head. *No?*

"This has to stop," she insisted. "I don't want this."

Yes, she did, and he wasn't past playing hardball to prove it.

Noah slid a pair of fingers into her panties and slid them right into her wet center. Immediately, they were drenched and scorched by her wet heat. She clamped down on his fingers, her sheath all but weeping to be filled.

"I think you're lying. You want this very much."

She whimpered as he teased her sweet spot with his fingertips. "My body does. But my mind... Stop that, please."

He stilled, but didn't remove his fingers.

"Why do you think you don't want this? Wednesday should have proven that I won't demand your love."

Lauren sent him a jerky nod. "I know. But it's unfair to both of us."

"Unfair?" Interesting perspective. He'd keep pursuing that...as he pursued his way deep into her body. "I have mind-blowing orgasms with you. Whatever is between us is so hot, it's off the charts. I don't feel short-changed. In fact..."

With a hurried sweep of his hand, her panties glided down her thighs, over her calves. Before she even opened her mouth to protest, the little scrap of white cotton hit the floor.

"I feel damn lucky. And hungry...for you." He wedged his shoulders between her legs.

"No. You shouldn't. You— Oh my God," she cried.

He raked his tongue through her drenched slit and settled right where she needed him. She was so damn wet. And swollen. Her soft folds pouted for attention. And Noah was all too happy to give it to her.

"No," she protested weakly. "Oh, I can't. I shouldn't…"

"Come for me, sugar. Let me taste you all over my tongue."

"But…but I—"

"Shh." He lifted her hips in his hands and brought her soft pussy right up to his mouth. His own personal feast. And where she was concerned, he was so fucking hungry.

He dived in, teasing her with a dart of his tongue around her folds, into her silken channel…but never quite reaching her clit. Delving between her lips, skimming just to the side of the hard knot of nerves that screamed for his attention, he brought her to the brink, put her on edge. Sweat broke out across her skin. Her thighs trembled as she clutched the sheets and closed her eyes, as if focusing on the sensations. Her ragged pants made him smile.

Backing away, Noah shrugged off his shirt and doffed his boots and pants in less than a minute.

The mere act of undressing gave her too much time to cool down and think with nothing but her insecurities and fears.

"Please…don't. We can't." Lauren sounded as if she were crying about that fact.

"We can. Look how easy it is…"

Naked now, he slid back up her body, parting her thighs wider and wider as he covered her completely. And with one determined thrust, he slid home, so damned deep into her swollen, grasping pussy, the sensations of her flesh, of coming home, tore a groan from his chest.

"Oh God," she wailed. "It feels so good." She squirmed against him. "But it's not right."

She managed to get the words out in a broken, panting whisper.

So slowly it made his teeth grit, Noah forced patience—even though he swore he had none left. "Why isn't it right? You're not attached. Neither am I."

He plunged home again, balls slapping against her ass. She gasped, and her body sucked at him greedily. Noah clenched his teeth. Damn, the woman set him on fire.

"But…" She struggled for breath once, twice. "Who do you think of when you're inside me?"

Crazy question. "You. Always you."

Another withdrawal that made her hiss in pleasure, another hard bump against her G-spot as he rammed deep. He could feel release boiling in his balls, barely under control. He rasped in a breath, then another. Damn, how was he going to maintain enough control to show her who he really was and help her understand how she really felt about him?

"I'm thinking of someone else."

Noah stopped. Dead stopped. A curse hovered on his tongue. Who? Who the fuck was she thinking of when he was buried balls deep in her? Who was the son of a bitch she wanted more than him?

His brain broke free of the lust-induced haze, and he remembered that Lauren didn't know who he was. Not right now.

Forcing himself to relax—and hoping he hadn't read the situation wrong—he pumped into her body again, once more, a light tease of flesh on flesh. Slow. Designed to inflame, not satisfy.

Her sex clamped down on him again. Much more of that, and she'd short-circuit his brain.

"Who are you thinking of?" he demanded. "You can tell me."

"I can't," she whimpered.

He teased her again with another friction-filled stroke and raised her need another notch. "You can. I'll pretend to be him, if you need it."

"No," she gasped. "I've been pretending. I want the real thing now."

Great news…if she was actually thinking of him, of Noah. "You think you can't come without him now?"

Even as she lifted her hips in invitation, conflicting words tumbled from her mouth. "I don't want to."

"I don't think your body is going to give you a choice." He filled her with ruthless strokes of his cock. "Neither am I."

The time for words were over. The time to strip her of control and learn the truth had come.

Fitting her hips into his hands, Noah lifted her to his cock and let loose, sinking into her with every hard inch, every bit of power he had. He dragged his head against the sensitive flesh inside just behind her clit, then slammed down, grinding against her, hitting the little knot of nerves on the outside, too. And he chanted her name, growling it in her ear, telling her how much he loved being inside her, how hard he wanted her to come.

She couldn't resist for long. Soon, panting, writhing, she tightened around his cock, her fingernails digging into his shoulders. She mewled and wrapped her legs around him, tightening…tightening until her pussy was like a vise on his cock.

Pulses fluttered around him, and Noah clenched his teeth to stave off his own need to come. She was close…so close. An indrawn gasp. Another.

"What's his name?" he demanded. "In your mind, who are you fucking? Who's going to make you come?"

Around him, she closed her eyes and her sheath fluttered again, harder. Then she clamped down on him in one wild beat and she screamed, "*Noah!*"

Yes. God, yes. She was thinking of him. She wanted him inside her bed, her body. Hopefully, her life.

By some miracle and a lot of grinding of teeth, he managed to hold off his own desperate need to come as he pumped her through her orgasm, which raged around him.

With a vicious yank, he ripped off the mask and rumbled, "Open your eyes. Open them!"

Her lashes fluttered up from her flushed cheeks, slowly raising. Her dark brown gaze fastened on his naked, moonlit face.

She blinked once. Again. Confusion filtered across her face, drawing her brows down in something near a frown. His heart pounded as he gritted his teeth and waited. Sweat poured across his skin as he forced himself still, fighting the urge—the instinct—to pound deep inside her until she acknowledged him. Until she accepted not just the lust, but the undeniable need and emotion boiling between them.

Then her face changed again. Finally, recognition. And with it, shock.

"Noah?"

She closed her eyes again, shutting him out. He felt her panic and an arctic chill sweep through her body, into him.

No. *No!* She was not going to do this, to close herself off from him. He's already endured ten years of watching, of wanting. Since the day he'd met her, on the day she'd married Tim, he'd done nothing but ache. She'd admitted that she thought of him when Mr. Mysterious possessed her body. Why would accepting the reality they were the same man upset her?

"Yes, Lauren. *Me*. Look at me."

He was still growling like her midnight stranger, and she responded to it, opening her eyes once more.

Their gazes connected, and he felt the electric connection all through him—in his gut, which clenched with anxiety. Down his spine, which sizzled with possibilities. Searing his cock, which hardened further at the thought of having her again. As himself. Always.

"Look at me," he snarled again, "while I fill you. Fuck you. Make love to you."

Shock still reverberated through Lauren's system as his insistent growl echoed around her. He filled her aching sex again, now so sensitive after her last orgasm. She gasped.

Noah. He was deep inside her now. *Noah.* All this time…

Noah.

Improbable. Impossible. How could Noah be Mr. Mysterious? But it appeared to be true, even if she couldn't wrap her mind around it.

Why was he here? Did he really want her? Was this just a quick, fast screw for him? But then why go to the trouble of inventing Mr. Mysterious, sneaking into her house…telling her he wanted to make love to her. That he did, in fact, love *her*.

"Oh my… I—I don't understand," she managed to get out.

"Yes, you do. You know exactly what I want."

She knew he wanted to come. The way he thrust into her again made that totally clear. He was so engorged, she could swear she felt every ridge, every vein, of his cock. The rasp of his steely shaft against the raw nerves inside her made her clutch at the bed, grasping the sheets in her fists. God knew that, greedy or not, she wanted to come again, too.

But did he want more? Everything she wanted…but was terrified to pursue?

"I've spelled it out," he clarified. "Explicitly. When I bound you to your bed and fucked you last Friday, what did I tell you?"

It *was* him. No denying it now. No imagining that Noah had just shown up tonight and magically figured out who Mr. Mysterious was and what he'd been doing to her. He knew…because he'd been there, too.

"That you wanted me." Her voice trembled.

"That I'd wanted you for years and I intended to have you."

He punctuated the statement by grabbing her hips and stroking deep inside her again. Deep enough to make her gasp. Her sensitive walls fluttered around him and heat burned low in her belly, under her clit, now pulsing in demand.

"When I spread you across your dining room table and let my cock feast on your pussy, what did I tell you then? Do you remember?" he asked, then filled her again with another ferocious stroke that burned inside her. A knot of need tightened unmercifully as he filled her completely again and again.

The pleasure finally compelled her to answer. "Yes. You told me you loved me."

"Exactly. Do you remember that, next, I climbed into your bathtub with you and held your head as you sucked my cock before I took you on your bathroom floor?"

How could she forget?

She tilted up to meet his next thrust, anticipating the jolt of need. It morphed into an ache beyond any she could fathom. Or handle. She raised her gaze to his face again. To him. She zeroed in on his eyes. His dark pupils dilated wide, ringed by that intense icy blue. Sweat beaded at his temples, rolled down his neck. He exuded feral masculinity as both his hands tightened and his shoulders bulged. He sank deep inside her, pleasure stealing across his angular features, sharpening them. That same pleasure ripped a possessive growl from his chest.

Resisting it wasn't possible, even when a thousand shining thoughts and hopes bombarded her.

"Lauren," he rasped, his voice on edge. "Don't look away."

Helpless, as if his gaze held her captive, she shook her head, but her stare never wavered.

He lifted her legs on either side of his hips, and she locked them behind his back, taking him deeper than ever before. Next, he reached up, cradled her face in his hands. The intensity of his eyes, the raw, scorching need burning from his gaze scalded her senses.

"For ten fucking years, I've wanted you. Waited for you."

Each phrase, he punctuated with another demanding thrust into her body, another nudge at her heart and soul. He stretched her wide, scraping every sensitive nerve in her channel. Her body trembled with need. Her mind spun. All this time, he'd thought about her? For the last week, Mysterious and Noah, the same man? That thought alone was enough to blow her mind. But to think that he'd wanted her for ten years…

He covered her mouth with his, and Lauren gave in to sensation, not having the will or the strength to resist. Just like his cock, his tongue slid deep, taking total possession. She was too aroused, too aware of this man, to refuse.

"I love you." He looked right into her eyes, pushed deeper into her body, as he said it. "I've always loved you."

His words illuminated every dark corner of her body, echoing through her heart. And she burst into a million pieces, exploding all around him, rocketing up to a hot swirl of stars, bright lights, and searing pleasure that slammed her with every pulse of her womb.

Noah tore his lips away and tossed his head back on a dark groan of pleasure, roaring as he filled her one last time and released inside her.

One look at his flushed face told her he'd not only given her pleasure, but his heart. A bit of his soul. That expression told her that he intended to take hers as well.

Lauren feared he already had.

Chapter Ten

Lying with her head pillowed on his chest, Lauren listened to his slowing heartbeat. Heavy lassitude wound through her limbs. Tangled together, she and Noah were both damp with a sheen of sweat. Bliss ran sweet through her body. Despite her best intentions, she'd fallen for him hard.

He was her mystery man. He'd been sneaking into her house, stealing into her body with torrid passion time after time. And those words of love he'd uttered just before her orgasm...totally stunning. The shock and disquiet punctured her lazy satisfaction. Euphoria slowly deflated.

Uncertainty blasted her when Noah turned his gaze to her, intent and questioning.

Lauren didn't know what to say. He wanted her to be happy about his revelation. To laugh and say yes to more. She wanted to...but wasn't ready for love and devotion with anyone, even Noah. Especially Noah.

He was all drive and single-minded intensity, all plans and strategic execution. He'd turned that dedication and ability on her...and if she wasn't careful, she'd be a goner. What was she saying? Where he was concerned, she already was.

Bad move. His declarations of love aside, it would only be a matter of time before he dumped her for a calendar model or some other twit who had more in her bra than her head. And where would she be? More alone than ever. Completely broken-hearted. No thanks.

Even knowing that, she couldn't quite let him go. She should and she would. But not yet. And no wonder. He could drive her to insane heights of pleasure. He was sexy, sharp, steadily employed, kind—everything she wanted. Good with her girls, fun to hang out with.

He claimed to love her, despite being three weeks out of a relationship with Misty and her silicone pom-poms. Was that possible? Lauren frowned. She had no idea. He *had* cooked up Mr. Mysterious just to get near her. Because he thought he loved her? Maybe. More likely, he'd done it because she'd been a challenge. Noah did love to take on difficult tasks and beating the odds. Maybe he saw her as his ultimate quest if he thought he'd wanted her for ten years.

She sighed, trying to process it all. Not happening—at least not in the next five minutes. What came next?

The question itself scared the hell out of her. The answer terrified her even more because she wanted to stay and give them a chance. But in the back of her mind, that voice... How long before Noah's something shiny and new—probably wearing a D cup and possessing great legs barely covered by a little black skirt—snagged his attention and permanently diverted him elsewhere, leaving her with a broken heart? Noah had such a long string of women, she could probably wrap it around Texas Motor Speedway—twice.

Wait. He'd already talked about another woman, the divorcée. Noah claimed to love that woman, too. If so, Lauren wondered why he was in bed now with her, professing his devotion? Damn, the bastard was emotionally two-timing her before the tingle in her orgasm had worn off. And he'd seemed so sincere when he spoke about loving her. Unless...

Oh, holy hell! *She* was the divorcée. He wasn't in love with two different women or cheating when he'd sneaked in, stripped her down, and buried himself so deeply inside her it was as if he tried to reach her soul. He'd been talking about her all along. In fact, he'd been talking to her—about her. Not just talking. *Lying* to her about there being another woman. And using her own advice to orchestrate her surrender.

A hot wash of anger burned away the last of her pleasant satiation.

She'd said she wanted excitement and a spicy sex life. He'd dressed up as Mr. Mysterious and given her pleasure—way beyond her expectations. She'd told Noah she wanted someone steady. He fit that bill, too. Lauren wanted someone good with her girls. He'd invited them to swim, grilled them some of their favorites, then made solemn little Emma smile. In short, he'd listened to every word she'd said and tailored a courtship just for her.

Hell. Put like that, Lauren wasn't sure whether to be stunned or flattered or pissed as hell.

She sifted through her memories of their conversations, and her heart stopped beating. Everything he'd told her he wanted with his fictional divorcée—marriage and babies and love... He'd said he loved *her*, but what did he know about love? What did he know about staying with a lover beyond the orgasm? Nothing.

She sucked in a ragged breath. A lasting relationship between she and Noah? No. Impossible. He'd get bored and leave her. That was inevitable. If a professional cheerleader couldn't hold his attention, how was a woman with ten additional years and pregnancy stretch marks supposed to manage? When he left, she'd have to deal with not just disillusionment, like after her marriage, but a gaping hole in her heart. No thanks.

Still, she couldn't help but wonder… He'd planned this whole seduction for how long? Weeks? Months?

"Lauren?" He rolled to face her, the sheets whispering intimately, like a lover beckoning. "Talk to me, sugar."

Talk to him, like bare her soul? No. Trusting anything he said would be unwise, but very tempting…

She looked away and swallowed against the hope and questions shining bright in his eyes.

Edging to the other side of the bed, Lauren put space between them and grabbed the sheet, covering every inch of her nudity she could. The scrap of linen didn't help much, considering he was laying on the rest. And didn't appear to be in a hurry to give her more.

"You planned this, didn't you?" Her voice shook. "The way you plan a-conquer-and-overcome strategy at the office. You laid out and followed through on the steps of this—this deception."

He frowned, then spoke softly, "I planned this, but not to deceive you. I did it to show you how I felt about you, in a way you wouldn't feel threatened by. You said yourself that you would have run like hell if I simply told you I loved you and wanted to be with you."

"Totally beside the point. Ask me out on a date, like a normal guy. Don't manipulate—"

He grabbed her arm. "If I merely asked you out and caught you at a weak enough moment to get a yes, you would have found a hundred ways to keep me at a safe distance so you wouldn't have to risk your heart."

"Because I'm not ready for this."

"You are," he disagreed. "I've waited and watched. I know you're scared but there's no reason. We're going to be great. We already are."

"No, and I don't think you're ready for this, either. You take the decision out of my hands and think everything is great? You make choices for me, decide who I have sex with, when and how? That's not great. That's not love.

"Next, you talked to me about pursuing a gun-shy divorcée. Oh, wait. That would be me. Duh! How silly of me to assume you were honestly asking me for advice with a genuine problem."

"So I didn't go about this the best way, but you being stubborn and stand-offish and needlessly afraid *is* a hell of a problem. Yes, I asked you for advice. Who better to go to than the source for accurate information?"

He still didn't see anything wrong with his strategy. Unbelievable. The fact he'd gone to all the trouble to ask her advice, to invent Mr. Mysterious, would be flattering if it really meant anything. But Noah didn't *love* her. Maybe he thought he did. The truth was, he loved a challenge more. And with her disavowals of love and their past, he'd likely seen her as his personal Mt. Everest.

She ripped her arm from his grasp. "I should have guessed. You plan *everything*, apparently including my seduction. Why didn't I realize before now that you were using the very advice I gave you against me to conquer me? How damn stupid am I?"

"Conquer? Damn it, Lauren. I'm not some frat boy who's looking for a locker-room boast and I'm not trying to ruin your life. I'm trying to love you, like I've been wanting to for ten fucking years."

Ten years? "That's not possible. I would have been married to Tim and—"

Shelley Bradley

"Exactly." He moved in, erasing her personal space, his chest against hers, their foreheads nearly touching. Then he anchored his hand around her nape. "It was hell watching him slowly hurt you, day by day, little by little, withholding the attention and love I was dying to give you. All I could do was sit by while he shattered your heart and illusions. Knowing you cried at night, betting your body craved what I was aching to give you, damn near ate me alive. I waited for you to recover, and these two years destroyed my patience and restraint."

Lauren had no idea what to say. His growl and the blast of heat from his blue eyes told her he believed every word he said. Stunned didn't begin to cover her reaction.

"In all those years…you never said a word."

"I couldn't. You were a good friend's wife. If I crossed that line— and don't think I wasn't damn tempted—you would have ended up hating us both for it. Remember the night Tim was out of town for your birthday a few years ago?"

One of the lowest points of her marriage. Tim had been gone for weeks. He'd flown home for two days, spent three minutes inside her body, an hour or two playing with the girls, then when she'd finished his laundry, he'd packed up and left again. And she'd cried for the lack of love in his touch, in his eyes. He'd been on auto-pilot, doing his duty, relieving his physical need. Moving on. She'd known then that divorce was imminent, but didn't have the courage to file. It would mean so much change…

The night of her birthday, Noah had come by and found her crying. He'd persuaded her to dress up, asked his mom to watch the girls, then taken her out. The place had been loud and crowded and so much fun. Exactly what she needed. A bottle of wine later, she'd realized she hadn't smiled like that in at least five years. She'd known then that she had to change her life.

166

Of course, she'd awakened with a colossal hangover the next day, but the resolution had remained. She followed through a few days later.

"I remember."

"That night, in the restaurant," he took a deep breath, and a muscle ticced in his jaw, "you looked so damn gorgeous. You smiled when everyone sang to you. You let me hold you close when we danced. I felt your heart race when I pressed you to my chest. I felt your hard nipples, too. That night, I could have brought you home and taken you to bed."

Lauren gasped and opened her mouth to protest. She swallowed it.

Though she wished otherwise, he was right. He could have had sex with her that night. When he'd smiled at her, the stirrings of attraction she'd felt over the years had blossomed. For the first time, she'd yearned to be a woman with him, rather than a friend.

Fast forward two years. Now, he was way more than a friend. This past week, she had been a woman with him, learned him as a lover, experienced the touch of his sure hands, the full thrust of his cock as he penetrated deep.

Despite her disquiet, she blushed.

"But if I had slept with you that night, you would have avoided me after the divorce. You would have dismissed me as a part of your past, written me off as a mistake, and made your new life without me."

Again, he was right. He understood her, deep down. It made her glow…even as it scared her to death.

"Walking away from you with just a kiss on your forehead…I don't think I've ever done anything more difficult. For a week, I second-guessed myself. And jacked off every damn night, fantasizing about having you in my bed, all to myself. I couldn't stop thinking about the sexy cleavage, the flash of leg, the hint of flirtation in your smile. But when you filed for divorce that next week, I knew I'd done the right thing."

Lauren bit her lip. She didn't know what to say.

"Since then, I've been keeping you close, waiting for you to recover and feel ready to date…"

He'd been keeping her close? Did that mean… She gasped as another betrayal loomed in her mind. "Oh my God. My job. You didn't hire me for my ability, but to fu—"

He slapped a hand over her mouth. "Stop there. I didn't hire you to fuck you. I wanted you on staff for your ability. I know you're wholly capable of your job, and you've proven it time and again. Danson and Martin both have said more than once they wished they'd hired you first."

Lauren stewed. Maybe that was true. Likely, even. She was damn good at her job and she knew it. "But the whole set up was awfully convenient for you."

"I won't deny that. I got a fabulous, hard worker and to spend my days with the woman I knew I wanted to spend my nights with, too."

It was overwhelming, so much to digest—if she could believe him. "How am I supposed to trust anything you say?"

He clenched his teeth. "I'm not the enemy."

"Are you sure? Because most of my pals don't deceive and manipulate me."

"Do any of them want to love you forever?"

She didn't answer that, and Noah cursed.

"This is bullshit." He vaulted off the bed with a snarl. "You know I'm not out to hurt you. My only goal was to make you realize something you were too fucking scared to realize for yourself: we belong together. And now you're going to dismiss everything between us because you don't like the way I went about it?"

"Did you think that manipulating and lying would make me believe that you love me and are ready to give up your collection of women for some happily ever after with me?"

"I thought we'd have a much better shot if you stopped deceiving yourself," he muttered, his voice rough-edged. "I still think that. I wouldn't have had to invent a non-existent woman to ask you advice about or dress up as Mr. Mysterious if you were willing to be honest with yourself."

"You're going to blame me?" Was he for real?

"Why are you upset? You wanted a lover, and we wanted each other. Oh, you made a great show of pretending you wanted our relationship platonic. I just found a way to let you feel how good we are together for yourself and stop denying the pull between us."

What he said made sense…in a twisted way. But that didn't make it all right. "And you thought deceiving me would do that? That's insane!"

That comment pissed him off, if his thunderous expression was anything to go by. "It's using the resources at your disposal. And it worked. You responded to me every time I sneaked into your house and made love to you."

"I didn't know it was you."

"Doesn't matter. You pretended it was me."

Noah had her with that fact. She'd moaned that very confession mere minutes ago.

Lauren pulled the sheet tighter against her breasts. Noah's logic was firing on all cylinders. It wouldn't be long before he started putting two and two together and coming up with something other than five. He was going to figure out that she more than liked him, more than wanted him. He'd take advantage of her tender feelings—until he got bored and left. He might think he was ready for happily ever after, but he had no practice in staying beyond the orgasm, not in a real relationship.

"That's a small point in the larger scheme of all your lying. I admit, I pretended it was you once or twice, for a moment or two. It doesn't mean anything."

"Now you're lying, too. You responded to 'a stranger' because you were thinking of me. I know how that game is played. And why it's played. It means something, sugar. Own up to it."

"It means I hadn't had sex in two years."

"But not just that. If you were thinking of me and wanting me, but avoiding me, there's a reason. It means you care."

"I do care. You're a good friend. But I feared sex would screw everything up. Turns out I was right."

"Friend?" he spat. "Yeah, I'm sure that's what you were feeling when your pussy gripped my cock like a vise and you came." His eyes narrowed. "What we have, it's more than friendship. If it wasn't, why did you start dressing sexier on days you knew we'd be together in the office? Why did you wear that perfume you know drives me wild? Was that all for Gary in Accounting? I used to believe that, but you know what? I think now you did that to get my attention. You wanted me to think of you sexually."

Oh, hell, He'd noticed her attempts to dress for him? He'd done a damn fine job of pretending oblivion. "Did I dress sexier? I don't recall that."

"Yeah, so fucking sexy, I could hardly look at you without salivating and attacking. And you just told lie number two."

He was right. She tried not to squirm under his direct stare. But that icy blue gaze told her that if she lied again, she wouldn't like the consequences. It also told her that he wanted her again.

Grabbing the sheet, Lauren drew it up to her neck and covered herself completely. Noah, on the other hand, stood beside the bed without a stitch on—and it was distracting the hell out of her. Every time he moved, golden skin and heavy ropes of muscles moved in fluid harmony. Hell, even when he took a breath, those corrugated abs of his undulated. And the longer her eyes stayed on his body, the more his cock engorged and rose until he was nearly at full staff.

Damn! All this mooning…it had to stop. But she couldn't deny that she wanted him again, that her body warmed and ached at the thought of inviting Noah deep inside her again.

No, no, no. Bad girl! Noah was a friend, her boss.

Yeah, and the man who knows every square inch of your body and can make you scream in unbridled pleasure. Even if you're afraid he'll crush your heart, he's the man you love.

Not a helpful realization.

Noah edged closer. "You dressed sexy for me. Admit it."

Reluctantly, she nodded. "A mistake on my part. Being attracted to you doesn't make having a relationship a good idea, however."

He merely grunted at that. "Just attracted? Tonight, you made love with me, not some pretend stranger. *Me.* You're not the kind of woman to respond with such abandon to someone you don't care about."

Oh, hell. He was on to her. "Noah—"

He moved so fast, he was like a blur, suddenly on the bed, in her personal space, pinning her to the headboard in the cage of his arms. "Look at me."

Lauren did, right into those blue eyes that always captivated her. There she saw worry and pain and a growing edge of anger. She couldn't have looked away for anything.

"Tell me you don't care about me as more than a boss, more than a friend. Tell me you don't love me."

She opened her mouth but couldn't say it. She couldn't look at him and lie. But admitting her love would only throw open the door to her heart and let in pain she could only imagine.

"Noah..."

"C'mon, you're on this honesty kick. I honestly love you. I have for years. I wanted you the first time I saw you. I was honestly willing to do whatever I had to do to make you mine."

"The ends justifies the means?" she asked tartly.

"Yeah. Don't change the subject. Look at me and tell me you don't love me."

Oh, she wanted to. Really wanted to. It would save her heartache and sanity. But she wasn't sure it was possible.

With a cry, Lauren pushed against his chest and tried to shove her way out of his embrace so she could escape to the bathroom. He grabbed her shoulders and held firm, pinning her to the headboard.

"Answer me." His gaze caressed her mouth in a hungry stare. Blood flowed through her body, engorging her nipples. The slightest look in her direction and she got all hot for him. Bad sign. Very bad. Her only consolation was that his cock swelled as well, rising full stuff and ready.

When he met her stare, he growled, "You get me hard. Just one look. And every time, I'm ready in an instant. You do that to me. Only you. Because I love you."

The demand in his voice made her tremble. God, it would be so easy to just give in and admit she loved him, too. But if she did that, she'd only be opening herself up to a broken heart from which she might never recover.

"You say that…" She frowned, trying to keep tears at bay.

"I mean that." He shook her, glowered, intent and determined.

Lauren shook her head. "Soon, your wandering eyes will follow someone shiny and new."

While her emotion would last way beyond an introduction to the next slick female who caught his eye. And his abandonment would kill her. Better to end it now and start healing than wait until she fell much deeper.

It just didn't feel that way.

He cursed, the word blunt and ugly. "We talked about this. I told you, everyone else has been a substitute for you. I can't even tell you how many women I dated because they looked like you. How many times I fucked someone with my eyes closed so I could pretend she was you."

Lauren gasped. The image of Noah with someone else made her stomach curdle. But to know that he'd pretended those women were her… She couldn't think, couldn't comprehend… As if he knew her incredulity, he kept talking.

"You told me earlier that pretending wasn't enough for you anymore. It hasn't been enough for me for years. You want me to be honest, here it is: I love you; I've always loved you. I want to marry

173

you, grow old with you. I want to spend my days devoted to you, every night inside you—"

"No, you don't. You think that, but you've never been faithful to one woman in your life."

"Because you were married, and nobody else mattered. Answer the question: do you love me?"

Lauren swallowed. *Yes. God, yes.* "It's not that simple…"

"Yes or no."

He wasn't going to leave until she answered. The firm grip of his hands and the demanding glint in his eyes told her he planned to be an immovable mountain. She'd seen him in business. In a game of corporate chicken, he never flinched, never gave in once he was determined to have his way.

And giving him the truth would only give him the power to keep pursuing her, until he cornered her, wore her down, and claimed victory.

The moments with him would be sublime. Dizzying happiness. Full of wild satiation and smiles. Incredible. Unlike anything she'd shared with Tim. Even more intense than fantasies.

But it wouldn't last. Noah was as domesticated as a Bengal tiger. Hoping she could housebreak him into the role of suburban husband was beyond insane.

It was emotional suicide.

In the fight between honesty and self-preservation, she surrendered her ideals and whispered, "No, I don't."

Shock passed over Noah's face before it hardened into something cold. He backed off the bed and reached for his pants, his cock hard—his eyes harder. "Damn it! You condemn me for lying so I could prove you have my heart. But you're quick to lie right to my face in order to protect your own."

Guilt and shame showered over her in a hot wash. He was right. Totally.

But that didn't change a thing.

She watched with stinging watery eyes as he thrust on his shirt and shoes, then stalked toward her again. Lauren tried to back away from the fury on his face. She didn't fear that Noah would hurt her. He wouldn't. She was terrified that he would touch her, overwhelm her. And he wanted to; it was stamped into the hard angles of his face.

He reached her, and with a sweep of his arms, he laid her flat on her back, directly beneath him. In an instant, his hard mouth slanted over hers, his harder body enveloped her, pressing her into the mattress, leaving her no question how badly he wanted her or how angry he was.

His rough kiss dominated—her senses, her resistance. His tongue swept through her mouth with familiar abandon, filling her with the flavor of his determination and need. His lips molded against hers. A low groan from his chest rumbled through her body and ripped through her self-control. Against her better judgment, Lauren melted into him, opened her mouth to him, and arched against the furious rise and fall of his hard-slabbed chest.

Desire didn't just spark inside her; it ignited into a firestorm. The blaze overtook her in an instant. Noah knew just how to hold her, kiss her... He'd learned her body too well. Touching him was exhilarating, terrifying—like she imagined skydiving would be—scary and stupid and a rush like no other.

As she reached up to sink her fingers into his hair and raise her hips to his, Noah tore himself away.

Shelley Bradley

Staring with accusing eyes, he backed away to the foot of the bed as his chest heaved. His fingers worked into fists.

"Fuck! You're willing to throw everything we could have away, every bit of the fire and need and love between us—"

"Noah." She reached for him, regardless of the fact she dropped the sheet, exposing her breasts.

His gaze dropped to the bared mounds, still swollen and berry-tipped. His nostrils flared, and he swallowed. But he didn't succumb.

"It wouldn't last," she said, cutting into the thickening silence.

"You're going to throw us away because you're too fucking scared to believe that I love you. Forever. You're telling me the crazy tactics I used to win you meant nothing. You think I'd do all that just to conquer a challenge or get laid? You think I'm too stupid to know what's been in my heart for ten years, or that I would jeopardize our friendship and working relationship just to get off? You're out of your fucking mind if you do."

Lauren didn't know what to say. He didn't understand. He couldn't since he'd never been abandoned or endured a divorce.

She'd wanted a fling, was too jaded to believe in fairy tales. And what he seemed to be offering was an illusion. It was too much, too sudden, too unreal.

"I think you believe everything you're saying, but the way you plan… You say I'm not just a challenge for you. Maybe not, but how do I know you don't have some grand checklist of life that includes acquiring a wife and kids? Now that you're pushing forty, maybe you're feeling…desperate to settle down and convinced yourself that I'm the one because I'm suitable and comfortable."

He looked at her as if she'd come from an alien planet. "I didn't pursue you because my biological clock is ticking. Marrying and having

176

babies with you has been on my list for years, but only with you. I want *you*."

"Noah, I don't think you really understand love or the realities of marriage. It takes more than good chemistry."

"I know that!"

"How could you? You don't exactly have the reputation for staying in a relationship."

He shook his head. "This is about you. You're painting me with Tim's brush and penalizing me because...why? You can't let go of your fear left over from the divorce. You're afraid to try again, and you're too scared to admit that you fell into bed with me because you fell in love with me. You keep insisting what we have is just fantasy because that's easy. The reality scares you, and you won't even try to accept it, no matter how big the reward. You simply refuse to deal with it. You bitch at me about lying." He cocked a dark brow, cynical fury burning in his eyes. "Look in the mirror, sugar."

Without looking back, he turned away and marched toward the hall, anger set in the taut lines of his shoulders and clenched fists.

He was leaving. Just like that, leaving. Panic welled up inside her at the thought, grabbing her heart and squeezing. "Wait!"

With a sharp turn, Noah pinned her with a glare. "For what? I'm not going to tell you to find me when you come to your senses. I've done my waiting, ten years of it. I'm not waiting a minute more."

Chapter Eleven

Noah spent Saturday drunk. Sunday was looking like a repeat.

Yeah, Lauren was willing to throw their relationship away over her irrational fear, but his grand scheme, his lies, hadn't helped. He'd fucked up. Big.

Clutching a bottle of Jack Daniels in one hand and bracing himself against the portal of the open French door, Noah stared out at the quiet morning hovering in a hushed mist over his backyard.

Just days ago, Lauren had been here, smiling, laughing. Her girls swimming and playing. The sense of rightness had screwed with his head, made him believe in a faulty plan. That had been his downfall.

Raising the bottle to his mouth, Noah chugged swallow after swallow of the liquid fire. The alcohol burned his empty stomach. A quick glance in a decorative mirror on the wall to his left told him he looked like shit—hair askew, two days' growth of beard, rumpled clothes, sunken, hollow eyes that echoed the sensation in his chest.

For a wild week, he'd had Lauren, held her, fantasized about everything from the taste of her cream to sliding a ring on her finger. After one sweep of his mask to the floor, it was all over.

Where had he gone wrong? She'd been interested in him at the office. Her discreet glances, sexy blouses, the glimpses of thigh-high stockings...they hadn't lied. He believed she'd been thinking of him, of Noah, when he sneaked into her bed and body dressed as Mr. Mysterious. He'd gotten drunk on the need in her intoxicating touch.

If he hadn't miscalculated...

Oh, hell. *If onlys* wouldn't help him now. Lauren was gone, probably forever.

On that cheerful note, the phone rang. Probably his mother. She'd been horrified when she'd stopped in yesterday afternoon to find him surrounded by two empty bottles of tequila and he'd confessed that he hadn't eaten since lunch on Friday.

With a suffering sigh, he reached for the phone on his belt. The caller ID surprised him. Not his mother...

"Yeah." He couldn't quite keep the rancor out of his tone.

After all, the man on the other end was one of the big reasons for his own torment.

"Noah, buddy. How've you been?"

Tim sounded a little too chipper for Noah's mood, particularly since he wanted to reach through the phone and beat the shit out of Lauren's ex. If the bastard hadn't neglected her and hurt her, she wouldn't have been so gun shy about getting involved.

"Busy." He barely sounded civil. "You?"

"Actually...not so busy. I've been backing off my work schedule some. Spending more quality time with the kids. They're growing up so fast."

That snagged Noah's attention. "You're not paying homage to the work god twenty-four/seven anymore?"

"No. Work isn't life. A lot of people tried to tell me. Hell, Lauren begged me to get that. Guess it took losing her and most of my friends to buy that clue. I don't want to wake one day to find my kids grown and hating me."

Noah's gut tightened. "You looking to get Lauren back?"

"No. She and I...we were good friends, but in the end, what we had wasn't enough for either of us."

Relieved, Noah exhaled, his mind racing. He lifted the bottle to his lips again and took a healthy chug. "Well...congrats on your balanced life." Or whatever. "What do you want?"

"Emma and Cass spent the weekend with me and told me they'd been swimming at your place a few days ago."

Yeah, the night he'd fallen hard and been delusional enough to believe Lauren loved him. Just before he'd bought into a flawed plan and fucked everything up.

"Yeah. They're good kids."

"Lauren has done a great job."

Noah grunted in response. Where the hell was this going? Tim wasn't usually big on the phone.

"Anyway," Tim cut into the silence. "Emma tells me that you and Lauren looked...pretty cozy that night. She got the impression it would have been quite the date if she and Cass hadn't been there."

Ah, the interrogation. No doubt, Tim expected him to dodge and play the game, work the information to his advantage.

At the moment he was too drunk—and too hurt—to do anything but tell the man what he really thought.

"No, it would have been way more than a date. I would have claimed her, pure and simple. Do you know I've been in love with your ex-wife since the day I met her?"

180

Tim hesitated for a long moment. "I suspected. The way you looked at her..." He sighed. "I never felt that way about her. Honestly, I expected you to do something about it years ago and give me an easy out of the marriage."

"*What?!*"

"Look, I knew for years I wasn't the man for her. I just didn't...want to hurt her by telling her I wanted the divorce. I encouraged you to spend time with her, thinking the inevitable would happen."

"It didn't. It never happened while you were married to her. Ever."

"Yeah." Tim gave him a hollow laugh. "I found out the hard way that for all your ruthless business strategy, you're an honorable bastard. But in the end, something happened that convinced her to leave me, so it's all the way it should be now, I guess."

"No, it's not," Noah growled. "You son of a bitch. Your neglect made her feel so unwanted that she's afraid to try an actual relationship with anyone, much less someone who would walk to the ends of the earth on hot coals for her."

"Ouch. I guess I deserve that."

"And more."

"Yeah... Well, you still want her. What's your angle?"

"I'm out of them, man."

"C'mon. You're the master of strategy. You can turn every situation to your advantage. You have contingencies for your contingencies. Knowing you, you've got some grand plan, and she won't know what hit her until she's fallen so hard—"

"It's over."

Hearing Tim's utter silence, Noah cursed into the phone. His head spun. Master of strategy? Is that how everyone saw him? Lauren had certainly cast him in that light.

Okay, so he planned his moves with as much precision as possible when it came to work. And yes…he'd done the same with Lauren. He hadn't known what else to do.

She'd accused him of methodically attacking their relationship like one of his execution strategies.

He frowned. Put in that light, the way he'd pursued Lauren sounded…ugly. Mercenary. Decidedly unromantic. Though he'd never gone to such lengths before, he'd used strategy to woo dozens of nameless women to his bed over the years. And she knew it.

Shit.

Tim's indifference had hurt her. But his own calculated plotting…that was just another huge reason she didn't trust him. Her refusal to be with him was, in large part, his own damn fault.

Just as he'd thought; he'd fucked up. Only now, he realized it wasn't a flaw in the plan, but the fact he'd made the plan at all.

He should have led with his heart.

Approaching her slowly, wooing her with flowers and attention and all the romantic stuff she'd never had in her life would have been a much better idea. Playing on her loneliness and using her own sexuality to seduce her hadn't been wise. He'd played pre-meditated dirty pool. He'd lied to her about pursuing a divorcée so he could ask Lauren how to win her and use her own advice on her…brilliant, devious—totally wrong.

"It's over?" Tim asked incredulously. "You're just going to give up? That's not like you. Maybe it would help you to know that after I dropped Emma and Cass off earlier, Lauren looked like she'd been crying. A lot."

No, that didn't help him. In the least. Hearing that only made something in his chest buckle.

He staggered back to the sofa and swore. "Why tell me? Why try to hook up your ex-wife with one of your buddies?"

"I owe her, man. I think you could make her happy. I just…never cared enough to try. Come up with one of your great plans, and I'll help you—"

"No."

He couldn't do it to her. Her residual fear from her marriage and divorce wasn't helping his cause. But he'd done the most damage, treating her like a challenge to overcome. The feelings and reasons had been so different, but he'd plotted her downfall as methodically as every other business strategy or sexual conquest.

He hadn't fucked up by being caught up in the emotion and revealing himself too early. He'd done that entirely by plotting so ruthlessly to start with.

"That's it? Just a no?"

"Just a no." Noah took another swig of whiskey. The pain of not being with her would eat at him, but he deserved it. Stupid ass.

"Seriously? You love her, right?"

"More than you can fathom, yes."

"You want to marry her. You'd be great in helping her raise the girls, and—"

"Yes, and if she wants all that, it will be up to her. But at this point…well, let's just say retirement will probably come before Lauren agrees to marry me."

Even though he downed another quarter of the potent whiskey, Noah couldn't drown out the reality of his words. He'd plotted, all right, believing like an asshole that he knew better and could push and cajole Lauren into the sort of love he felt.

Idiot. The only thing he'd done was earn a lifetime without her.

CR CR CR

Two weeks had passed. Two miserable weeks. And on a muggy Friday afternoon, Lauren was ready for the weekend.

The office had been busy. Very busy, and she'd purposely arranged her schedule that way. If she was focused on her projects and deadlines, she couldn't be reliving her last night with Noah and wishing things between them had ended better, second guessing herself and wondering if there was even a tiny possibility that Noah actually loved her. Work gave her an outlet for her buzzing, dazed mind, thank God. Unfortunately, nothing had distracted her from the ache in her heart.

The Monday after her blow-up with Noah, she'd nervously returned to work only to hear that he'd volunteered to spend the week in their downtown restaurants, which he never did, to work through some "ongoing issues".

In other words, avoiding her.

Later that day, she'd requested a transfer to Danson's management team. If Noah really loved her, as he claimed, would he just let her go? It was a test, perhaps a juvenile one. But Lauren was so in need of a sign from him—something to convince her that she mattered. Noah was too good a strategist not to realize that if she spent any significant amount of time with him, she would surrender, not just her body, but her heart and soul.

Within hours, she'd been notified that he had approved the request.

That little faxed scrap of paper had nearly crushed her.

He'd released her without talking to her. Without asking why. Without fighting for her, for them. Hell, without blinking.

He had turned his back on her, exactly as he'd done Friday night.

Well, now she had an answer. Lauren could only infer that she'd been right all along. Noah probably didn't love her...even if his speech and righteous anger, when she'd pondered them later in her lonely bed, had been convincing. But he'd let her go to Danson's team in a jiffy, apparently pining for...what? All of ten minutes?

To top it off, he was punishing her because she knew he wouldn't do fidelity for long and she'd called him on it. Okay, so she did have residual fear from the divorce, as he accused, but that didn't change the simple fact that Noah wasn't the marrying sort. She simply wasn't setting herself up for future failure with a man for whom fidelity was a four-letter word.

So she'd moved her cubicle over to Danson's part of the building, taking her suburban expansion project with her. She hadn't seen Noah at all in the last two weeks. Small wonder, given the fact she'd attended all the focus groups during that time, extracting the statistical and empirical data. The results were exciting. Now it was time to present her recommendations to the management team—including Noah.

In the past, Noah had finessed Danson for her. He'd talked to Martin and the others. He'd always paved the way for her success, looked over her presentations before she'd given them, offering suggestions. Like everything, he plotted and planned, never leaving anything to chance or anyone else's judgment.

Not with her, not this time. Now, she was on her own, the project and its outcome totally in her hands.

It felt good. And scary. Worst of all, knowing she was going to see Noah for the first time since that terrible night in her bedroom made her heart weep with pent up need and regret.

Lauren swept through the double glass doors of the conference room, entering the room with all her files and equipment. Danson waited at the head of the table with an encouraging smile. She tried to smile back.

Noah, sitting just on the right, distracted her. The pull of his heavy presence hit her. Thick air. Utter silence. She felt his eyes all over her, assessing. Devouring.

Lauren looked away and tried to keep her hands from shaking. There was enough gossip about why she'd switched management teams so abruptly already. No need to feed the rumor mill…even if she was desperate to look at the man. Ached to touch him.

And yearned to believe he loved her.

She had it bad. Really bad, waking up in the middle of the night in a sweat, body aching for something only Noah had ever given her. Once the dream ended, she just missed…him. His tousled hair, the smile in his blue eyes, the way he'd held her.

Gone. It was all gone. For the better, she kept telling herself. If she hadn't put an end to it, how long before he would have planned his next seduction, and she wouldn't have been his target? That would have flattened her heart.

What if he'd meant what he said that night, for real? What if she wasn't just a challenge or a checkmark on his list? What if he truly, genuinely loved her and had waited a decade for her?

Lauren stole a quick glance at Noah. She couldn't resist anymore. And still he stared, unflinching, unyielding—looking deeply unhappy.

Was it possible? Could he really have been unmoved by hoards of cheerleaders and models, and been utterly fixated on her? God, she wanted to believe...and yet fear swallowed her words every time she thought about telling Noah that she loved him.

"Ready?" Danson asked, breaking into her thoughts.

"Just about."

Lauren focused on her presentation set up, determined to chase away stubborn thoughts of her former boss.

As soon as they were ready, Danson hit the lights. Lauren started her PowerPoint slides, passed out her materials, and gave her spiel. She believed in this project and how it would help the restaurant chain. Her confidence projected, she knew, as she fielded questions. A thoughtful expression crossed Martin's face. He'd always been her big detractor, and so far, he'd yet to utter a single "voice of reason" comment.

She avoided eye contact with Noah. But still...she felt the heat of his stare.

At the end, Danson asked her to step out. Nervously, she curled her fingers into fists and exited.

The five partners gathered around the table, and she surreptitiously peeked at their interaction. From his expression, it seemed obvious that Martin voiced a concern. Big surprise. Danson countered. Gilbert nodded. Miles commented. Martin shrugged, as if conceding a point. Danson added a few words. A moment later, her new boss rose to call her back in.

Noah hadn't said a word. Not in the project's defense. Not to vindictively crush it. Not to plan whatever angle suited him best.

He'd said…nothing.

With her insides jumbled like the contents of a blender, Lauren entered the conference room and sat, nervously folding her hands in her lap. She glanced at Noah. She couldn't help it. His face gave away nothing.

"Lauren," Danson started, "we've talked it over as a team. The research is spotless and the results obvious. Your presentation made the uncertain seem inevitable. We've decided to go ahead with your full recommendation. We'll pursue three new sites, two north of downtown, one further west. We'll go for the print and radio blitz, participate in local community events to spread the word—the works."

Triumph beat a harder drum in her with every word. She'd done it. Somehow, in the middle of all her tumult and worry, she'd managed to get beyond her inexperience in this business, put together an idea that worked, and persuade five savvy restaurateurs to go for her proposal. And she'd done the last, crucial step on her own, without any of Noah's interference or planning on her behalf.

Amazing!

"Congratulations," Gilbert said, offering her his hand.

"Thanks, sir."

"If you're ever looking to switch management teams again, call me first next time."

"Hey, hey," Danson protested. "No thieving of employees. Back off."

With a laugh, Danson packed up his stuff and headed for the exit. The others followed suit with a good-natured chuckle. Lauren rushed to get in behind them. Gravity had nothing on the pull of Noah's presence. With him standing so close, she'd never forget the feel of his mouth on hers, stop aching for the way he made her body feel, cease remembering the shredded torture in his voice when he'd told her he loved her.

What if he really did?

Noah stopped her with a hand on her arm. "Wait," he whispered for her ears only.

"You lucky bastard," Gilbert murmured to Danson as he approached the double glass doors. "Noah's loss is your gain."

"Absolutely true," Noah called, wearing a plastic smile.

She barely heard with her attention so focused on his fingers wrapped around her arm. Even that small touch burned. What the hell would she do if he kissed her, burst into flames?

"Better luck next time," Danson joked, pushing the heavy door wide.

Within moments, they were all gone, leaving Lauren and Noah alone in the conference room. She squirmed under his intent stare, wishing he didn't look so beautifully familiar and she didn't know how wonderfully pleasure-filled and full of feminine power he could make her feel. She looked away. It would be so easy to touch him, confess her feelings to him... But unwise.

"How are you?" she asked to break the silence as she pulled discreetly from his grip.

He let her go without a fight. "It was a great presentation, Lauren."

Noah sounded like a colleague. Nothing more. And she hated that professional note in his voice. It was stupid and contrary, but she wished he hadn't just let her go, that he would go caveman and demand her response... Or tell her one more time that he loved her. Even if it wasn't true, the words made something inside her sing.

What if it was true?

Crazy. Noah wasn't built for commitment. She knew it. Hell, everyone knew it. Their parting was for the best.

It just didn't feel that way.

Now that she looked at him again, really looked, Noah appeared exhausted with dark-smudged and hollowed eyes. And, despite his Mr. Professional voice, he looked resigned. Dismal.

Was he…upset about things between them? Noah never mourned the end of a relationship; he just moved on. Most likely, she was reading too much into it. Maybe something else was bothering him.

What if he really loves you? a pesky voice in her head asked.

"Thanks. I learned a lot about preparing and making these presentations from you." It was the truth, and she owed him a lot for her success today.

"You pulled this one off all by yourself."

"Yes," she whispered. "I noticed that you didn't participate in the group decision."

"I didn't plan or strategize. I understand that you needed to complete this on your own, without my interference."

He'd figured that out? And acted completely against his own instinct to make her happy? Wow. Why? Why would he bother to curb his instincts, unless…

What if he actually does love you? There was that little voice again.

"Thanks. I'm happy about the outcome."

He nodded, but pain laced his expression. "That's all I ever wanted, for you to be happy."

Really? Then why lie to her about his identity when he was buried deep inside her body? Why manipulate? Why not just shoot straight?

After years in business the strategizing came naturally to him. Soul-baring honesty didn't. That was just him.

Maybe he'd been telling the truth, that he simply hadn't known another way to make her see him as something other than a boss or Tim's buddy. Maybe he looked so very unhappy now because he'd gambled his heart…and lost.

Maybe he really does love you.

The very thought made her tremble, weak-kneed. Her belly fluttered, her breathing tight. If he really loved her and she'd turned him away…

Lauren swallowed. *Oh God.* "Let's just…leave it."

"All right." His voice sounded like sandpaper on gravel.

Stupid, irrational disappointment hit her like a punch to the belly.

He raised a hand toward her, then curled it into a fist and dropped it to his side. "Can I say just one thing?"

"Yes." *Please do!*

But what if he started talking? What if he had some new plan and she fell for it and then, once she was settled and trusting, used his lies to cheat on her with Miss Decade Younger and—

What if he really loves you?

"For what it's worth, I'm sorry. If my attempts to bring you closer hurt you, I never meant for that to happen. I spent so many years in love with you, and I was afraid you never saw me as a lover. I wanted you to experience me, us, without pre-conceived notions. I wanted you to have the kind of love and passion I know you didn't get in the past. You deserve all that with someone who cares about you more than…" He frowned, his jaw hardening, as if he was having trouble getting the next words out. "More than his next breath."

His little speech cut her off at the knees. Despite her confusion and self-talk, Lauren felt her insides melt. Her eyes welled with tears. *He* was that someone, his speech implied. He cared that much. He'd devised a whole new person, probably spent hours deciding how to approach her, persuade her, seduce her. He'd sent her tantalizing gifts, notes that revved her libido. He'd made love to her like a man with nothing but her on his mind.

None of that would have ever occurred to Tim. Ever.

The reminder that Noah had done it all just to win her knotted in her belly, wrapping dangerously with her heart. And maybe...she could have him back again, if she just had the courage to say three little words.

Lauren opened her mouth—but fear smothered them again.

"I went about everything the wrong way, and I'm sorry."

Again, he lifted a hand to her as if he wanted to touch her. Again, the fist curled, his jaw tensed, his brows drew down in a pained frown. He dropped his hand.

Her heart broke with how badly she *wanted* him to touch her. And how much she feared losing herself to him, only to lose him to someone shiny and new. And it hurt. Better to hurt a little now than have a gaping wound that would slowly bleed the life out of her later.

"Apology accepted. I'm sorry, too. I didn't handle the other night very well. I never meant to hurt you, and I realize the things I said probably screwed up our friendship forever. I hate that."

"Just don't hate me." His voice cracked, and he swore.

Grief hung on his heavy expression. Her heart flipped at the sight, and she reached out, despite the voice of caution screaming at her, and took his hand.

Lauren fought against tears. "I could never hate you." *Not when I love you so much...* "For what it's worth, if you truly love me, then I'm the biggest idiot in the world."

He threaded their fingers together and squeezed like it was a lifeline. "You still doubt that I love you?"

She sucked in a harsh breath. How did she answer that one? Put it into words? She could hardly sort through the tangle of her thoughts.

At Noah's belt, his cell phone rang, shattering the quiet intimacy of the moment. He swore in an ugly four-letter word that told her in one succinct syllable the depth of his frustration.

At the moment, she didn't disagree.

"I think you mean it today. Tomorrow...?" She sighed and shook her head. "Let's not put ourselves through this."

Noah turned off the ringer without looking at the caller ID even once, something else Tim would never have done. He focused on her. Nothing but her.

He sighed and nodded, both heavy with resignation. "If that's what you want. But I do, you know. Love you. No matter what you think, I always will."

ଔ ଔ ଔ

"He what?" Kat screeched in Lauren's ear.

Lauren sighed into her cell phone as she navigated through dicey traffic on Central Expressway as she left downtown Dallas. "Don't make me repeat it all because I know you heard me. The Cliffs Notes version is that Noah was Mr. Mysterious. And there is no other woman. He was just pumping me for information. He lied to me about the whole thing."

"All this happened two weeks ago, and you're just now telling me?"

"I was trying to figure it all out in my head. Sorry. What am I supposed to make of it? On the one hand, I felt lied to and manipulated...and even though it's probably stupid, oddly flattered. On the other hand, I just don't see him as a suburban husband and father, not when he's used to a new model every month. But what if he really does mean it?"

Kat hesitated. "He said he did all this because he loves you."

"Yes." He'd said it more than once, in fact.

"And that doesn't phase you at all?"

"You mean like make me ooey-gooey inside? A little." Okay, more than a little.

"But you don't believe him?"

"I don't know what to believe. But even if he does, given half the chance, Noah might barge into my life with all the subtlety of the bulls charging at Pamplona. He plans everything, and that would include my life."

"No offense, hon, but you could use a little help in the planning department. You don't even make plans for Christmas until the week before. Maybe you could...um...balance each other out."

"Kat..."

"I'm being serious. Is that really your hang-up here? His planning fetish?"

The way Noah did things, all dominant male take-charge attitude, turned her on. A lot. She got wet just thinking about the sensual plans he had made when he seduced her, his elaborate plans to drive her to the edge of her self-control and push her over while she screamed his name. That totally turned her on. Everything about him did...except when he was lying.

"No, that's not my biggest fear. He'd plan stuff in my life, yes. And maybe I could use that, provided he wasn't lying. But how would I pick up the pieces after he planned the selection of his next girlfriend?"

Kat sighed. "Okay, look at this objectively. He lied. That's a pisser, but he didn't do it to hurt you. He did it to *win* you."

"That's his side of the story."

"I doubt he was lying about that. Why bother? Noah might have a reputation for being a playboy, but he's never been a deceitful jerk. I know you. If he told you flat out that he loves you, you wouldn't believe it. Just like now. You'd be afraid to believe it. If he told you that he wanted to marry you, you would have run screaming in the other direction. What sort of options did you leave him?"

"You're taking his side?" Lauren felt her jaw drop. Wasn't Kat *her* sister? Didn't blood give her some advantage here?

"Just think about his choices before you get all high and mighty. You wanted him, but you were willing to let it go because you didn't want to say anything, right?"

"Yeah. It was awkward. He's my boss and Tim's friend and... It seemed like there were too many obstacles. I didn't think he'd be interested, and I didn't want to be hurt."

"Noah wanted you so much, he worked around awkward, got up off his ass, and put himself on the line to be with you. He risked his pride to lay his heart at your feet. Think of everything this man did to get your attention, just to touch you..."

Lauren had thought of it. Repeatedly. The reality swam in her head, drowning out anger, leaving her with nothing but a hollow ache. Giving in...it was so tempting. With a few words, she could have that amazing man in her bed, his eyes gleaming blue fire, charged by wicked lust.

But... "That doesn't excuse lying."

Kat scoffed. "It goes a long way. Stop being righteous. You hate the fact he was more clever than you and outmaneuvered you. But his lying isn't the issue, not really."

Frowning, Lauren gripped her steering wheel, wishing for a moment it was her sister's neck. "Okay, that's true, but—"

"You're scared at the lengths he'd go to in order to win you."

"A little," she admitted. "But it's like a thrill ride, too. I know that doesn't make any sense..."

"No, it does, honey. But I think the thing that's really got your panties in a twist is the fact he's making you confront your fears about the future and marriage. You're afraid that you'll give him your heart and he'll leave you someday."

In stop-and-go traffic, Lauren stopped and chewed on a ragged nail. An uncomfortable resonance in her brain and tightness in her stomach told her that her younger sister was right.

Discomfort at facing those very fears warred with guilt in her belly. She'd rejected a sexy, intelligent man with deliciously wicked intentions to avoid facing her own demons. She'd hurt him, desolated him, if she could believe his expression after this morning's meeting.

Damn, she felt like a coward. But that didn't make the fear go away.

"Bitch. I hate that you know me so well. So what are you suggesting?"

"Get over this little tantrum before you piss away the best thing that's ever happened to you."

"The best thing? You never liked Tim."

"With good reason. Look, you divorced the bastard because he never paid a lick of attention to you. Now, you have a man willing to blanket you with affection, devote night after night to your happiness and pleasure. And you say you're pissed about the way he approached you. Besides being way too picky, you're lying to yourself. You're just afraid of getting hurt."

"Gosh, Kat. Don't mince words. Tell me what you really think." Lauren rolled her eyes.

Her sister just snorted. "You need to stop thinking less about how a new relationship might be painful and think more about what kind of happiness you might be passing up if you let this stupid-ass fear run your life."

Kat's cutting voice—and the truth—whacked her across the face. Her sister was right. Noah was the anti-Tim—supportive, attentive, able to focus on their relationship. There was just one little, D-cup-or-better problem…

"Okay, you're mostly right. But there's something else you don't understand."

"This better be good."

"Seriously, Kat. I'm like…Mount Everest to him. It's the challenge, not the person. Once he's scaled me and planted his flag, it'll be over."

"Sounds to me like he's already planted his flag more than once."

Lauren rolled her eyes. "Stop. I meant metaphorically."

"You think he's so hard up that he needs to ruin a decades-long friendship just to get laid?"

Um, put like that? Well…no. That didn't seem Noah's style. But…

"Kat, I've watched him with every other woman he's dated. I've seen the same pattern over and over. Once he thinks he's got me, he'll be bored and restless and leave me. Knowing that, it's hard to just 'get over' my fear."

"You need to consider three things: A—He acted that way with *other* women, women he wanted to be you. He's not using you as a substitute for someone else. If he's pined for ten years, chances are cupid has maimed him for life where you're concerned. B—You cut him loose at the expense of your heart because, get this, you're afraid of being without him and hurting. Hmm. Hello, is logic home?"

"It's not that simple—"

"Yeah, it is. And don't interrupt. C—You're looking for guarantees in a relationship before you sign on. Gee, if they all come with one and I didn't know...color me stupid. Here I thought relationships were about learning to trust and respect one another, sticking it out in good times and bad, and hoping for the best along the way. But gosh, if they come with guarantees of not being cheated on and left, sign me up."

"Now you're just being sarcastic."

"I'm being right. I'm also hanging up now. Before you get the kids and get busy, while I know you're stuck in traffic and have nothing else to do, I want you to think about what I said. Noah loves you. I believe the guy. Why shouldn't you? You're crazy about him. It's a great chance to start all over and do things right. The future... Well, what's that cliché, it's better to have loved and lost than never to have loved at all? I think that applies here. Gotta run. Ta ta..."

Click.

Ugh! That was just like her difficult, opinionated sister.

God bless her. Tears seared the backs of Lauren's sleep-deprived eyes as she mentally sorted through Kat's words.

Noah loved her. Lauren couldn't run from that fact anymore. Instead, an insidious part of her heart embraced it like a warm quilt on a chilly winter's day.

She loved Noah. They knew each other well, respected each other's senses of humor and quirks. Undoubtedly, he'd drive her nuts a time or two along the way. No doubt she'd do the same to him.

Cutting him out of her life now...it *was* crazy. The weeks without him were killing her, like a dull, rusty blade in her chest coming closer and closer to destroying her heart. She didn't want to be without him. If their relationship ended up being a short one, well, at least she'd have memories. If she left him now, she'd have nothing but regrets.

Lauren already had plenty of those, and they sucked. She wasn't settling for regrets anymore.

She picked up the phone again and hit one of her speed dial buttons. "Hey, Mom. Are you busy tonight? You're not? Great! Would you mind if the girls' came to stay with you? I need to visit a...friend."

Chapter Twelve

Friday fucking night, and he was alone. And home by ten-thirty. How the hell had it happened?

When a certain sandy blonde with flashing dark eyes had let him into her life—into the sweet, honey-wet depths of her body—substitutes had ceased to work.

She'd captured him completely, without even trying. She had simply been herself, and for ten years, he'd ached for nothing else. After a brief week in paradise, Lauren had kicked him out. Largely his fault, yes. But she'd bashed in his heart and snipped his balls when she'd walked out the proverbial door. He'd started a million plans in his head to win Lauren back before he had to remind himself scheming was exactly what she didn't want. Damn it.

God knew he wasn't lacking other offers. Just tonight at his former hot spot, some young blonde had all but humped his leg like a puppy in heat. In the past, he'd been able to muster up enough interest, especially if the blonde had lush curves and chocolate eyes and a husky laugh that went straight to his cock. Like Lauren.

Now...nothing. He'd danced with the blonde tonight, knowing he'd have to get back in the game at some point. He'd tried to pep talk himself into sleeping with her. Nothing doing. Holding the woman—

Jessica? He couldn't remember—everything south of his belt buckle may as well have been dead. Tonight's blonde had been too skinny, too young, too…loud and obvious. Self-absorbed. Misty had been much the same. As had a long line of blondes before her.

Noah sighed as he let himself into his huge, rambling, terribly empty house. Lauren was gone—and not coming back. He'd sell the house eventually. Why did an eternal bachelor need four bedrooms and three baths? The wife and kids he'd wanted for a decade weren't moving in anytime soon.

On that depressing note, Noah felt his way through the dark, into his living room and made his way down the hall.

Bed. He'd go to bed. And probably jack off. Again. Thinking about Lauren, her supple curves all spread out on his bed, bound and wet and ready and all his.

Now he got a reaction from parts south. Sighing, Noah looked down at his stirring cock and shook his head. Jessica and her artificial D cups rubbing against him had done nothing. One thought of Lauren, and every inch he'd sworn was dead suddenly sprang back to life.

"Picky bastard," he muttered to his dick as he approached his bedroom.

The door was closed. Odd. He never closed his bedroom door before leaving the house. Only made the room stuffy…

But he was running on next to no sleep, and the pressure building up in his balls was nearly enough to strangle him. That, coupled with the constant ache right between his pecs, was really distracting the hell out of him.

Tired, Noah groped for the knob and found a piece of paper taped to it.

Scowling, he pulled the paper free. What the…? Had someone been in his house? Who had keys? Mom. His administrative assistant, Jennifer. He couldn't see either of them leaving a note taped to his door, rather than leaving a voicemail.

After flipping on the light in the hall, he unfolded the paper and read…

You. Me. Naked skin. Shared fantasies. A whole night.
Now.

His heart dead stopped. Those were the same seductive words he'd used, more or less. Taped to his bedroom door. Not written in his handwriting.

But in Lauren's.

Holding his breath, he shoved the door to his bedroom wide open.

His jaw dropped at the sight that greeted him. His cock leapt to full attention.

Lauren stretched out on his bed. Ankles and one wrist bound. Writhing like she needed him to ease her ache. Now. *Holy shit.*

She was here? Here! *Breathe*, he admonished himself. *Goddamn breathe.*

Her hair tangled in a wild honey-sweet cloud, teasing her neck, toying with the swells of her breasts and her swollen rosy nipples. She was blessedly, beautifully naked…except for a little black mask. Golden candlelight bathed every seductive valley and ripe swell, every inch of her soft, sun-kissed skin. *Son of a… Whew!*

Legs spread, Lauren's bare sex glistened for his gaze. Advertising. Luring. Calling out to him. His fingers, mouth and cock all twitched with the urge to answer. *Fucking torture...*

"Hi, stranger."

Her voice, sultry, thick with arousal, wrapped around his cock, stroking it to a painful length. Noah gritted his teeth and tried to make his brain work, to sort through why she might be here, naked and available, taunting and so fucking gorgeous. But his brain wasn't working. It just registered naked Lauren and reacted like a hungry dog with a steak.

"You've got five seconds to get off the bed and get dressed," he growled, "before I shove my cock inside you and fuck you so hard, you'll spend half the night screaming your throat raw."

Lauren didn't move a muscle, except to send him a kittenish smile that added another jerk to his cock. Damn it, the woman was playing with a book of matches in the midst of dry kindling, sprinkled with gunpowder and topped with dynamite.

"Promises, promises," she purred.

She wasn't just inviting; she was *taunting*.

The strategist in Noah knew he needed to rein in his lust, ask why she'd come, where she saw their relationship headed after the fabulous fuck she was goading him into. If he gave in, she might just well leave after her orgasms. He'd be tipping his hand, showing her exactly how much power she had over him. He'd have no bargaining chip when the night was through.

The man in him only cared about getting inside her sooner than now.

"Yeah," he growled, stalking closer and toeing off his loafers. "One I *will* deliver on."

His tight black T-shirt came off in a second. His jeans in about two. He leapt on the bed, insinuating his body between her legs. His tongue thrust deep at the same moment his cock did. He thanked every god he could think of that she was wet enough to take him in one plunge.

Lauren gasped. "Noah!"

Home. Perfect. Mine.

He moaned, the sound tortured, guttural. Had anything ever felt this good?

Ravenous for her taste, her smell, her touch, he dove into her, submerging himself. Hard strokes of his cock, punishing lashes of his tongue. He sank deep, deeper. It wasn't enough. It never would be.

Her one free hand plowed through his hair, clutching at him as she tilted her hips, mewled, and invited him even farther inside her.

"Yes." The sound tore from his chest as pleasure shot through his body.

The intense penetration aroused him, but it was being inside Lauren, knowing she'd come to him, would soon come with him, that was boiling his blood, scalding the need building up inside him.

But he needed something…

Without missing a beat, he jerked the mask from Lauren's face. She blinked, those long lashes fluttering at him, even as her pussy did the same around his cock. Her brown eyes melted as she looked up at him, focused, not looking away. Her gaze lay bare. Vulnerable. No anger, no fear, no reticence. Only acceptance, giving. Total surrender. That look reached inside him, ratcheting up his desire to feral levels, tugging on his heart until he thought it might burst.

Lauren was destroying him. Not little by little, but in great, big gnawing hunks. And still he needed more.

The scarf. The one tied around her left wrist. It had to go.

With a mighty tug, he ripped the offending black wisp away. He didn't know where it had come from and he didn't care. He only knew both her hands were free.

"Touch me," he pleaded, voice harsh against her mouth. "Hold me."

"Yes!" she shouted, folding both arms around him, holding him tightly against her as he propelled his way into her tight, clinging sheath again. Again. Again. Until he wanted nothing else. Could think of nothing else.

"Noah." His name fell from her lips in a pant.

He didn't answer. He couldn't. Instead, he gripped her hips, tilted her up even more and fucked her wildly.

God, she was killing him. The head of his cock dragged across her sweet spot. She clamped down on him, gripping, sucking him back in, even as her arms held him tight, as if she'd never let him go.

Lauren fisted his hair in her hands. "Noah!"

"Why...did...you...come...here?" he demanded, one word between each thrust.

She cried out and pressed her lips to his.

As much as he wanted to lose himself in the dizzying flavor of her mouth and that intoxicating kiss of hers, he wrenched away.

"Why?" he growled.

She was panting now. Every breath a harsh exhalation that ripped through the thick summer air each time he shoved his way into her broiling depths. Her pussy squeezed him hard now. Harder. Jesus, he was going to lose his mind. The ecstasy was building up, heavy, an irresistible ache. He sucked a harsh breath between his teeth, trying to hold off his orgasm long enough to make her come.

But first, he wanted a goddamn answer. He'd seen it on her face, but he had to hear her say it.

"Why?"

"I need you," she sobbed.

"For a fuck?"

She shook her head. When she trembled against him, body taut with need, Noah looked down into her dilated, expressive eyes. She was on the edge, nearly ready to explode. But everything she felt was still shining at him, and he thought he might explode even before she said the words.

"For always. I love you."

That was all it took. The head of his dick dragged against her sweet spot one more time, and she convulsed, thrashing, crying out, his name a chant.

No way he could resist that. He wasn't even going to try.

Pleasure slithered down his spine, gathering into a boiling pool of need in his balls. With a last thrust, the ache burst, shooting through his entire body as he stiffened, plunged, shouted, and clutched Lauren like a lifeline as he drowned in a sea of ecstasy.

Moments passed. They drifted into minutes, broken only by slowly regulating breaths and heartbeats. Still, Noah didn't move, remained lodged inside her sweet body, his arms around her. She'd come back—and he would find some way to keep her if she thought for even a second about leaving.

But Lauren's arms remained around him, fingers stroking through his hair, gliding down his sweat-slicked back. She pressed a kiss to his shoulder, his jaw, the corner of his mouth.

His cock stirred with interest again, like he was nineteen, not thirty-nine. Only Lauren could do this to him, damn her. She'd better not think of leaving again.

The string of kisses she continued to gift him with said she was in no hurry to go anywhere. Her mouth fell softly on the blade of his cheekbone, the damp skin at his temple. Her teeth tugged on his lobe.

"Noah?"

He closed his eyes. What did she want? Hell, he'd given her the power in this situation. Given her exactly what she wanted. What if he'd imagined the tenderness in her eyes? What if her declaration of love was nothing more than heated passion talking?

"Why did you come here?" Noah barely recognized his own voice. Scratchy. Rough. Ragged.

"Not just for sex. The last few weeks have been miserable without you."

"You kicked me to the curb and told me I was a scheming bastard."

She kissed his cheek. "When you let me finish the expansion presentations without help...I knew you understood that I didn't want you planning my life."

"I got it. But you didn't believe that I love you. I don't know how to convince you not to be afraid. What I want...it hasn't changed, sugar."

"Thank God." She smiled up at him. "You have my sister to thank for making me realize that I was leaving you because I was afraid of being without you. Which, as she pointed out, makes no sense."

"But now you're willing to take a chance with me?" His heart started to chug, beating faster with hope so desperate he could taste it.

"If you're going to get bored and leave me the way you have Misty and every other woman—"

"It won't happen," he swore.

Solemn-faced, he stared down at her, forcefully penetrating her gaze, willing her to understand. "Tonight, I could have had a woman named Jessica."

Instantly, she struggled beneath him, doing her best to dislodge him.

All that wiggling with his cock in her sweet heat only served to stir his cock to full length. With a slow glide, he pushed back into the depths of her body, all the way to the hilt.

"Damn it," she hissed. "Get the hell off—"

"I said I *could* have had her. I didn't say I did." He thrust again slowly, his erection sliding through her like a hot knife through soft butter. "Truth is…" he withdrew unhurriedly, then pushed his cock back in at the same pace, maximizing friction, "…I wasn't even remotely interested in a woman tonight until you came here."

Again, he treated her to a lazy thrust. *Damn, this better be arousing her.* The slow burn of her flesh over his was searing him.

"I wasn't interested in sex without you," he clarified. "Seeing her boobs half exposed in a low-cut shirt all night did nothing for me. A mere thought of you…and I was so hard I couldn't think straight."

He thrust again, at that agonizingly measured pace.

Beneath him, Lauren moaned, "Noah." Her stiff body lost some of its starch.

"That's it, sugar," he chanted on another smooth glide. "Get it through your head; there isn't going to be anyone else. I've wanted you for ten years. You told me the last time we made love that substitutes weren't enough for you. They're definitely not enough for me. They never will be again."

"Noah." As she called to him, tears welled, spilled, ran silver down her cheeks.

"I want to marry you," he whispered, stroking into the wet heaven of her wet slit again. "Have babies with you. Hell, I bought this house for us."

"You—you did?" To say she looked shocked was like saying the Yankees had a few fans. "But that was…a year ago. More than that."

"That's when I started to hope that maybe we could work this out. If you don't like the house, we can sell it and move—"

"I love the house." She hesitated, bit her lip shyly. "I love you."

He had to have her now, wrapped around him, all his. Scooping her up, Noah came up on his knees so she straddled his lap. Then he reached back and tugged away the bonds around her ankles. Lauren wrapped her legs around him immediately.

Clutching her in return, he maneuvered his way to his back and settled her astride him, right over his cock. He sank deep through her slick folds, right against her cervix. She gasped.

Oh, this was one of his favorite positions. Not only did it feel damn fine, it was easy to get a woman off over and over…and watch the whole show. And he'd never made love to Lauren in this way.

Noah wanted to change that. Now. But…

"I've said my piece, sugar. I hope you know I love you." He pushed a wild tangle of tawny hair away from her flushed face and ran his thumb across her swollen lips. "But it's up to you. Are you staying? Or going?"

"Oh, I'm staying. You can't get rid of me." A smile broke out across Lauren's face as she eased up on his cock, then back down. He gasped.

"I'd never want to. I've never loved a woman until you. I waited for so long, wanted you for years..."

Smiling, she leaned in, brushing sweet, swollen nipples across his chest. When she wriggled her hips and writhed over him again, Noah sucked in another sharp breath.

"I have a naughty little secret," she said, then put her mouth to his ear and whispered, "I wanted you for years, too."

He paused. "Years?"

"Since before the divorce. I've been in love with you since the night you took me out for my birthday and didn't take me to bed."

Lauren had loved him for over two years! Thrill slid through him, tingling across his skin. The sensation spiked straight up to euphoria a moment later. Another pistoning of Lauren's hips, and he added ecstasy to the mix for a sensation so exquisite, so powerful, so unlike anything he'd ever felt with any other woman, Noah had to grit his teeth and grip her hips to stop the climax rushing through him.

But when she pulsed and fluttered around him, crying his name in a high-pitched scream, he couldn't stop the unstoppable.

Orgasm hit Noah with all the subtlety of a freight train. His arms flew around her, holding her close as he arched up, as deep inside her as he could reach. And she took him, gasping, her pussy milking him in hard clamps in an agonizing blitz that seemed to last a blissful eternity.

After a few quiet moments, his heartbeat calmed. His breathing slowed. And he couldn't stop smiling as he angled their bodies to the side of the bed and reached into the drawer of his nightstand.

Lauren lifted her head with a sated groan, her cheeks flushed, her lips swollen, her hair wild. She'd never been more beautiful.

Through slitted eyes, she saw where his hand was reaching and frowned. "If you're reaching for the condoms...um, it's too late, I think."

Noah just laughed. Grabbed what he wanted in his big palm, and shut the drawer. "I'm so happy you're here."

"No place else I'd rather be. No one I'd ever rather be with," she whispered.

The words went straight to his heart.

"Make me even happier," he murmured, staring straight into her chocolate eyes that all but melted him with her warmth. "Marry me."

He opened his palm and produced a small box.

Lauren's eyes widened. Her long gasp stopped his heart. Shit, was he moving too fast again? Planning too much for her?

"Sugar, don't panic." He closed his fist, hiding the box. "No rush. We can take it as slow as—"

"Are you kidding? We've wasted too much time as it is. Yes!" she squealed, then leaned down to pepper his face with kisses.

The sound reverberated through him, echoing with joy. He sighed, relaxed. Exhaled.

Everywhere she touched him was wet, and he gripped her shoulders and sat her up so he could see her face. Happy tears doused her cheeks. Noah brushed them away with his thumbs.

"You're sure?" His chest tightened with an anxious ache as he waited.

She nodded happily—and cried some more. "Yes."

"Don't you want to see the ring first?" He opened his hand again, right under her gaze.

Lauren glanced at the little black box, then again at him. A reproachful smile crept across her face. "When did you buy this?"

Noah couldn't hold back his sheepish expression. "The day your divorce was final."

"Pretty sure of yourself, Mr. Reeves."

"Pretty determined, soon-to-be Mrs. Reeves. If you don't like it, we can find something else."

But as she lifted the lid and was nearly blinded by the ring's beauty, she acknowledged that Noah had fabulous taste in just about everything—clothes, wine, food…a wife, she thought with a giggle.

"Have you already picked our wedding date, location, florist, caterer—the works?"

A laugh of pure happiness rolled out of him. "I have ideas, but if you'd like to plan it, sugar, you're welcome to."

"Wow, that's very…accommodating of you."

He grabbed the ring from the box, slid it on her finger, and pressed a soft kiss to her lips. "I learn. Slowly sometimes. But I learn."

"And what do you want in return for all this magnanimous behavior?"

He cupped her cheek and delved into her gaze. "To love you. For you to love me back. The rest, we'll plan together. Think you can handle that?"

A long, sigh-filled kiss later, she murmured, "I do."

About the Author

To learn more about Shelley Bradley, please visit www.shelleybradley.com. Send an email to Shelley at shelley@shelleybradley.com or join her newsletter via the link from her website to hear more about new and upcoming titles.

What would you do?

Trophy Girl
© *2006 Melani Blazer*

You're a NASCAR fan...pretty into it, thanks to your dad. You know a lot about the drivers, the tracks, the cars. Even though you try not to, you hear the rumors and see the off-track interviews. You know the reputation of the series champ, bad-boy Zander Torris. You know he's devastatingly good looking, and charming to boot, but with a different piece of voluptuous, blonde eye candy on his arm every weekend, you have zilch respect for him.

The only good thing you see in him is that he's a very generous benefactor for the camp where you're a nurse volunteer.

So when he walks into your clinic, unannounced and unexpected, and asks you—girl-next-door, unglamorous you—to that evening's benefactor's dinner, what do you do?

Hint, he's not taking no for an answer, so be ready at 6…

Available now in ebook and print from Samhain Publishing.

Samhain Publishing, Ltd.

It's all about the story…

Interested in writing for us?

Samhain Publishing is open to all submissions and seeks well-written works that engage the reader. We encourage the author to let their muse have its way and to create tales that don't always adhere to trends. One never knows what the next trend will be or when it will start, so write what's in your soul. These are the books that, whether the story is based on "formula" or an "original", are written from the heart, and can keep you up reading all night!

For details, go to http:

www.samhainpublishing.com/submissions.shtml

Samhain Publishing, Ltd.

It's all about the story…

Action/Adventure
Fantasy
Historical
Horror
Mainstream
Mystery/Suspense
Non-Fiction
Paranormal
Red Hots!
Romance
Science Fiction
Western
Young Adult

http://www.samhainpublishing.com

LaVergne, TN USA
07 April 2011
223290LV00003B/94/A